Jade Cameron

DARK RIDERS of OATH

(Book II of the Freedom Rider Trilogy)

A prequel to
FREEDOM RIDER
(Book I of the Freedom Rider Trilogy)

Order this book online at www.trafford.com
or email orders@trafford.com

Most Trafford titles are also available at major online book retailers.

Printed in the United States of America.

ISBN: 978-1-4269-0358-8 (sc)

Trafford rev. 11/16/2010

 www.trafford.com

North America & international
toll-free: 1 888 232 4444 (USA & Canada)
phone: 250 383 6864 • fax: 812 355 4082

To Marty, for his continuous love and support.
To my sons Justin (Angela) & Nick (Mandie),
and my beautiful granddaughters Annika & Alice.
To my sisters, family and friends.

But most of all, to my sister Debbie.
"You have shown faith, strength and courage over the last few years
in your fight with cancer. I am honoured to be your sister."

chapter

1

BOSS QUICKLY GRABBED the bags off of the table and threw them into a nearby cupboard. He pulled out his *Browning M. 1903 9mm* handgun from inside of his vest.

George Gomez, a new member of the club, also known as 'Whiskey,' had left the building forty minutes prior to Boss and Spud's meeting. Boss had finally accepted that George was reliable and worthy enough to receive his vest and first patch. George had successfully completed a ten-day operation with some of the other members of the club.

Spud and Boss stood quietly for a few more minutes, waiting for some sound or sign that they were not alone.

Boss took a deep breath and finally said, "I'm going in!" He raised his index finger to his lips as if to quiet Spud, because he knew Spud would have said something otherwise.

It was dim inside the building. They usually refrained from turning on unnecessary lights if they weren't in the other rooms; however, there was enough light to cast shadows if someone happened to walk by.

Spud stayed close behind Boss, in case he should run into trouble. The foyer door was slightly ajar. Boss' throat tightened while he attempted to swallow. There was no doubt now that they weren't alone.

Boss moved his empty hand backwards and instructed Spud to move into the darkest area of the foyer. Boss followed him. They stood still for a few moments. Whoever had come in through the front door was not in the foyer but possibly somewhere else in the building. Boss wasn't sure what they should do now. He turned to face Spud, but he also kept an eye open to his surroundings.

"I'm not sure what to do," Boss said, hoping that Spud might have an idea. Keeping his voice low, he continued. "How many do you think came in?"

Spud's guess was as good as Boss'. He had no idea. "Did they have a key?" Spud asked, as he looked towards the front door.

"I don't know. I guess that would help us figure out if they are a danger or not," Boss said. "Stay here." He quietly crept to the front door while staying away from the direct light. He scanned the door jam for any sign of damage; there didn't seem to be any. He glanced over at Spud again. For all they knew, the intruders could be outside by now.

Boss pulled the edge of the dark curtain away from the window beside the door, so that he could see outside to the parking lot. He spotted a couple of motorcycles in the distance. They were too far away to make out if they were familiar or not. He instructed Spud to join him. Spud went over and Boss moved aside.

"Do you recognize those bikes?" Boss asked, as he pointed.

"Hmm, not really," Spud said.

Loud voices were suddenly heard down the hallway from where Boss and Spud had entered the foyer. They ran back to the corner. Boss aimed his handgun towards the doorway. Spud was starting to hyperventilate. His hands were shaking as he tried to steady his pistol. "We're going to die, Boss!" he said in a panicked voice. "I knew we shouldn't have brought the drugs here. I just knew it!" Spud was losing it, and Boss needed him to get a hold of himself before he joined him.

"Spud, we aren't going to fucking die!" Boss tried to assure him. He looked at Spud sternly and noticed his trembling hands. Boss needed to take control of the situation. He pushed Spud aggressively into the corner and instructed him to stay low.

"But B-b-o-ss, you're ... gonna ...," Spud stuttered.

"Stay put," Boss whispered. He walked towards the voices. The hallway was clear. He breathed a deep sigh of relief. Turning the corner at the end of the hallway, he saw the backs of two men disappear into another room. He noticed the patch on one of their vests; it was the core patch for 'Riders of Reason.' Boss turned as white as a ghost. He raised his handgun and hollered extremely loud, "What the fuck are you idiots doing in here!" The men quickly turned around. It was Road Rash and Outcast, two members of the club in which Boss was the 2nd Officer. Road Rash swallowed the mouthful of beer that he had just gulped and then clumsily dropped the bottle. It smashed across the yellowed linoleum floor.

Spud heard the yelling and ran into the room behind Boss.

Boss quickly turned around. "Go and lock the front door. I'll deal with these two men."

Spud was relieved that the intruders were members of the club and not anyone else. He wiped the sweat from his brow and hurried back to the front door to secure it.

Boss aggressively pushed his way past the two bikers. "Clean up that fucking mess. I want to see you both in my office in ten minutes!" he hollered.

The two bikers were in major shit. They knew they weren't supposed to enter the building by the front door, unless it was for an emergency. Boss went into the back room and slammed the door. He was appalled with the men that they would disregard the club's rules. Boss realized it could have been because of the booze. Either way it was unacceptable.

Spud returned and walked up to the two bikers. Road Rash was moping up the mess on the floor while Outcast quietly leaned against the wall. Outcast let out a loud belch. All Spud could do was shake his head. He didn't dare say anything to the men, at least not before Boss had gotten his words in. Spud walked around the men and in through the door to where Boss went. He closed the door behind him and locked it. Boss was pulling the bags out of the cupboard and placing them back on the table. "I can't believe those two!" he suddenly said. "What has gotten into them?"

Spud sat down across from him.

"For now, let's get this shit locked up properly," Boss suggested. "I don't want to prolong this any longer. As soon as we can, we need to get rid of it."

Spud helped Boss put the bags into the large safe, which was hidden inside of a closet. Boss turned the dial until the combination secured itself.

A few minutes later there was a knock on the door. Spud waited for the okay from Boss before he let the two men in. The stench of booze filled the room when they entered. The men sat down at the table.

"Well, what do you have to say for yourselves?" Boss said sternly.

Road Rash looked over at Outcast and then back at Boss. "Hey man, we just forgot." He slumped in the chair.

Boss reached across the table and got a firm grip of Road Rash's T-shirt. He pulled hard and upwards until Road Rash was suddenly back on his feet; his chin resting on Boss' fist. Boss glared into his eyes. Road Rash gagged as he tried to swallow. He knew better than to fight Boss off.

"Don't you ever, I mean ever, cross me again!" Boss unclenched his fist and Road Rash dropped into the chair. Boss sat back down. He knew the men weren't in the best of shape, so there was no point drilling them too much because they probably wouldn't remember.

"Your keys!" Boss instructed, and he held out his right hand.

The men fumbled in their pockets and then placed their keys in Boss' hand.

Boss closed his hand around the keys, and then pointed at the door. "Now get out! I'll let you know when you're welcome back!"

Spud was quiet throughout the meeting. Boss was one you didn't want to mess with or get on his bad side.

As the two men started to leave the building by the rear door, they heard Boss' voice behind them. "And pick your motorcycles up when you're fucking sober!"

The door slammed behind them.

Boss tossed the keys into a nearby drawer. "They'll have to earn these back!" he said gruffly.

Spud spoke up. "I can't believe they were daft enough to come through the front door. Do you think they were up to something?"

"I don't know, Spud. At least now they have no access to the building. One more daft move like that and they'll be down the road."

Road Rash and Outcast had been members of the club for over a year now. They weren't the sharpest tools in the shed, and Boss had a soft spot for them. He met them at a motorcycle rally, and they had seemed distraught and distant. Boss took them under his wing and taught them the ways of the club. Mostly, they were sent out to do the easiest tasks. Boss had ulterior motives when he brought them into the club. He needed these types of men; ones that never expected anything in return. They both worked at a 4-pump gas station as their day job, and spent their downtime playing pool at the local neighbourhood pub. They drank too much for Boss' liking, but he figured it was the only way they knew how to release their frustrations.

They never talked about their home lives, families or anything personal.

Boss trusted them for who they were. They seemed to be very grateful for what Boss had done for them. The two men didn't enter the club with nicknames, so over time Boss watched and carefully came up with names that suited them.

Road Rash was medium height, about 5'10", and normally wore T-shirts, baggy jeans and the same ball cap every day. Boss figured he only owned a couple pair of jeans and four shirts at the most. Road Rash was about 180 lbs. and middle-aged. One could tell he experienced trauma through his younger years. The various scars that were scattered on his face, hands, and arms proved it. Boss never asked questions regarding them. Along with his many scars, Road Rash was overwhelmed with freckles and moles. This came with being a redhead. Road Rash was also known for being clumsy, even on his motorcycle. When the club rode together, Boss insisted Road Rash ride at the back of the pack, so that if he dumped his bike, no one else in the group would go down. He wasn't clean-cut and was not big on shaving or taking care of himself. Boss could barely stand near him for any length of time because of the unpleasant smell.

Outcast was the opposite of Road Rash. Boss couldn't figure out why they got along so well. Outcast was a handsome 6'2", 210 lbs., and quite fit for a man in his early fifties. He usually wore buttoned-up shirts, jeans and cowboy boots. He was a pleasant and quiet man, unless someone pissed him off. He was very intelligent, but his self-esteem was what suffered the most. Boss guessed this was one of the things that attracted Outcast to Road Rash. Road Rash would feed off of Outcast's insecurities, and this would help Outcast feel as though someone cared; unfortunately, Outcast wasn't able to see the big picture. He took care of his physical hygiene the best he could. His salt and pepper coloured hair was always combed neatly, and he would tend to overuse aftershave. Boss wasn't too worried because the smell would cover up Road Rash's displeasing odour most times. Outcast at least showed he had some perception of how he looked and smelt.

Observing the pair of them was like watching teenagers in adult bodies. Boss took their personalities and appearances with a grain of salt. They both had good hearts and dedicated themselves and their lives to the club. Boss couldn't ask for more. Members were hard to find who would commit like they did.

Boss had to reprimand the two men from time to time throughout the year, but never did he have to take their keys away. He felt bad and hoped that they would learn from their mistake. It was for the security of the family that they abide by the club's rules.

Boss glanced down at his watch. "Well, I think we should call it a night."

Spud agreed. "You bet, Boss. Are we getting rid of the stuff tomorrow?"

Boss nodded and flicked the light switch. As they left the building, he locked the door behind them.

chapter

2

THE DUST IN THE DISTANCE was a common occurrence to Marcus and Pablo, while they slaved in the field along with the labourers, under the intense heat of the afternoon sun. It was mid-April and quite hot in San Rafael, Argentina at this time of year. They had almost left it too late in the year to pick the grapes, many of which were on the ground dehydrated. Marcus, the oldest of the two boys, glanced up as he heard the rumbling of the familiar 1940 Harley-Davidson Knucklehead hard tail, which exhibited a Springer front end and ape-hanger bars. It was gliding down the dirt road towards their farm. Marcus looked over at Pablo and smiled. Their Uncle George had been away ten days this time, and the boys missed having him around the farm.

George was 6'1" and seemed much taller when he stood, as he always held his head high with confidence. He was in his mid-forties. He grew up in Mendoza but preferred the small town of San Rafael, where he now lived. He was soft-spoken and usually only talked when he thought it was necessary. He would rather sit and take the information in, then to talk someone's ear off with nonsense. His hair was white and short, and he proudly sported a complimenting beard and moustache, which he kept well-groomed. Family was important to George, and he grew very fond of his nephew, Marcus and step-nephew, Pablo. They were like sons to him. He watched and guided them through the years as they grew from young school-aged boys to teenagers.

A few years prior, George had moved in to assist Marcus' dad, Bernardo, whose wife lost her battle with lung cancer. A year later, Bernardo met Rosalia and her son, Pablo. Rosalia and Bernardo got married and then she and Pablo moved in.

Marcus was now sixteen years old. He was a lanky adolescent about 5'8". He had dark brown shoulder-length hair, which had a tendency to cover his eyes. His step-brother, Pablo, was two years younger. Pablo took pleasure in being clean-cut, and was taller than Marcus by a couple of inches. He had much lighter characteristics. He supervised Marcus while their dad and uncle were away. Marcus may have been older, but his mentality was much younger. He needed Pablo's guidance because he had been known for getting into trouble. Marcus was very fortunate to have him as a step-brother. Although only step-brothers, the boys grew and loved each other as real brothers.

Bernardo worked away from home for a month or two at a time, so it was up to the boys to carry on with the farm duties. It was a huge responsibility, and their education suffered because of it. Thankfully, in the last few years, their uncle was nearby for the most part. Pablo questioned his momma countless times about their dad being away, but she didn't have a response. This made day-to-day life at the Gomez's extremely stressful.

As much as the boys desired, they did not rush back to the farmhouse. They understood that their uncle needed time to unwind before they bombarded him with questions. They nodded at each other and continued with their chores.

George rode his bike up towards the back porch. With his left foot, he lowered the kickstand. Once the bike settled on the ground, he dismounted. He quickly removed the leather vest he was wearing, because he had neglected to take it off earlier and didn't want anyone to see it. He took his keys out of the ignition and hurried to the barn, where he kept the majority of his private things.

The door to the barn was open, so he knew the boys were still out in the fields. George shut the doors and wandered to the rear of the barn, when he noticed it was cleaner than usual. A smile crossed his face. He knew the boys could be trusted. He reached the back of the barn and pushed aside a heavy crate that was covering a trapdoor. Once the crate was moved, he reached down and unlocked it. He tugged up on the corroded handle and raised the trapdoor carefully. Then he pushed it upwards. He headed down the wooden steps, while lowering it behind him as he descended. Fragments of wood crumbled off of the door as it settled. He fumbled in the dark for the lantern that he knew was hanging to the left side of the wall. He removed the glass cover and used his lighter to ignite the wick. Suddenly, the area below brightened.

"Ahhh, just as I left it." He sighed.

He reached down and opened the wooden box that was next to him. He dropped his vest inside. His name patch 'Whiskey' was facing upwards on the back of his vest. His first name was in a smaller format on the front of the vest. For anonymity reasons, the club refrained from using their last names. He felt it had been a long time coming, but now, he was officially one of them. He finally felt as though he belonged. George clutched a bottle of rye that was laying in the corner of the box, opened it, and then took a big swig. Afterwards, he sat and rested on top of the box. He wasn't sure how much longer he could continue with this secret. His brother, Bernardo, wouldn't be pleased. George was concerned that he may have to leave the farm if his brother ever found out. He had been told by other members of the club that he was to keep everything hidden and wasn't permitted to tell anyone anything. He stood up after a few moments and brushed off his jeans; he was a mess. After many days of not being able to shower or clean up, one could smell him a mile away. Rosalia, Bernardo's wife, wouldn't approve. He hung the lantern back up and blew out the flame. Once he climbed up the steps and reached the top, he glanced around to make sure there was no one else in the barn. He secured the trapdoor and pushed the crate back over it.

Rosalia was busy in the kitchen preparing lunch when she heard George's bike pull in. She knew he would be starving. Bernardo was still away working. She had inquired a few times as to why he had to be gone for so long, but it always backfired to the point of almost ending their marriage. She didn't want this for the boys; she had to keep the family together. She had made a huge sacrifice, and because of it, she allowed her own dreams to die. Most of her acquaintances thought she was wrong in doing this and that no husband should treat their wife the way Bernardo treated her. He wasn't always this way; it was only the last few years. No one in the city of San Rafael knew what Bernardo did for work.

While Rosalia continued washing the potatoes, she glanced out of the window towards the field. She noticed the boys having a rest beneath the overhang of the run-down shed. She was proud of them and the way they were handling everything. Rosalia knew that because of their ages, it was the toughest time of their lives, never mind having to take on the obligations of the vineyard as well. She was appreciative of having such caring sons and didn't know what she would do without them.

Pablo called out to the workers in the field, but they didn't hear him. He got up on one of the trucks and gestured with his arms back and forth; this was an indication that they were finished for the day. He jumped back down and assisted Marcus in loading up the rest of the barrels, so they could take them over to the barn where another company would pick them up and take them away to the winery. After the truck was loaded, they headed over to the barn to park the truck. Some of the other workers would meet them there to unload them. Marcus and Pablo could never do this alone, and they sure didn't want to continue with the vineyard when they were older.

George wasn't sure when he would be called upon again, but he hoped it wouldn't be too soon. He needed rest and felt as though he had been on the go for the last three months. He still had savings to live on for a while longer, so he would be able to help out on the farm. Rosalia had her hands full with the boys, and George felt bad about having to rush off at a moment's notice. When he initially joined the club, he never envisioned it would take so much of his time; now he knew different.

He was hungry and exhausted. The boys would want to hear all about his adventures but that would have to wait until another day. He would have to be careful about what he said to them and not mention the club. He opened the back door and saw Rosalia standing near the sink. She looked mighty fine, especially after he had been with filthy bikers for ten days; she always looked appealing to him. He had a secret adoration for her and wished she wasn't married to his brother.

Rosalia looked up from what she was doing. She speedily dried her hands and hung up the tea towel on the handle of the fridge.

"Hey there, handsome," she said. The complexion in her cheeks radiated a pleasant shade of pink. "It's been a few days, hasn't it?"

"Hey, Rosa." George always called her that. He went over to her and gave her a tender hug. She returned his affection.

"Yes, and I hope I'm around for a bit," he said. "I'm going to go put my things away."

"Great," she said. "Lunch is almost ready. Oh, the washroom is that way if you need to clean up." Rosalia pointed and then giggled as George glanced her way.

After George cleaned up, he proceeded to his bedroom on the main floor. He walked into his room. Rosalia always ensured his bedding was clean and his room tidied before he arrived home.

It was a quaint little house. The exterior was a rustic wood design; the interior had wood floors throughout, two bedrooms on the main floor, and two conjoined rooms up in the loft. The sitting room was very small, but comfy, with a small woodstove in the corner which set off a warm feeling. To the right of the sitting room was the kitchen. The cupboards and counters were also made from wood and painted a rose colour. Rosalia often dreamt of a much larger kitchen. The back door opened to a small back porch, where five stairs led to ground level. To the right side of the house was a smaller door, not a legal exterior door, which led down into another room. The basement was mostly a crawl space, but had been extended near the back stairs for laundry facilities. Off the laundry area, was a small cellar where they stored their perishables. There were plenty of single paned windows in the house to allow the natural light in, which helped, so they wouldn't need to use too much electricity. The main house was a bit crowded for the five of them, but they managed with what they had.

He sat down on the edge of his bed, but he knew if he laid down, he would be out like a light.

The boys suddenly rushed in through the back door.

"Boys!" Rosalia hollered, and then she pointed at their boots.

"Shit!" Pablo said. He turned around and pushed Marcus back out to the porch. The boys removed their boots and brushed themselves off to make sure there was no dirt on their jeans. They went back into the house and apologized.

"No problem, boys," she said. "Now get cleaned up. Lunch is ready."

The boys went into the bathroom to wash up.

Marcus called out, "Where's Uncle George?"

"He's getting settled," Rosalia said. "Now hurry up!"

When the boys finished, they sat down at the table. Their Uncle George was already at the table and appeared to be half-asleep.

"Hey, Uncle George," Marcus said, "how are you?"

"Great, Marcus." He glanced up at the boys and smiled briefly.

Rosalia placed the food on the table. "Here you go." She sat down beside George and watched as her hungry crew dug in.

"So, how long are you home for?" Pablo asked, as he reached across the table for the Pollo (marinated chicken).

"Not sure, Pab, but hopefully a while," George said. "I know you boys have been waiting patiently for my return."

Marcus couldn't help but smile. He thought highly of his uncle.

There was a lot of talking while they were eating, which made for a late night. Rosalia didn't mind though, as she thoroughly enjoyed seeing George and boys together.

When they finally finished their meal, the boys got up from the table and cleaned the kitchen, but not without being sidetracked by a bit of horseplay. It usually took them a good hour to finish.

While the boys were busy in the kitchen, George disappeared into his room. He lay down on his bed, and as he predicted, he was fast asleep.

Rosalia spent the next hour lost in thought. She had mending to do on the boys' clothing, but she wasn't able to concentrate. She gazed out of the window into the distance, and wondered about her husband and how she would handle things if and when he ever returned. She didn't dwell on it too long, as thoughts of George were consuming her more.

When the boys came into the room, it broke her train of thought. She glanced up at them. "You boys better get some sleep," she said.

They went over and gave her a hug goodnight. "Night, Momma," they said, and they headed up to the loft.

"Night sons," she said and watched them disappear around the corner. She turned in shortly after.

Marcus woke abruptly to what he knew was the roaring sounds of a motorcycle. The sun wasn't up yet, so he thought that he may have been dreaming. He lay there for about twenty minutes but wasn't able to go back to sleep. Eventually, he crawled out of bed and went down the ladder to the main floor. His momma was in the sitting room. She glanced up from the book she was reading.

"You're up earlier than usual," she said, as she turned the book over on her lap. "Is everything okay?"

Marcus rubbed his eyes. He noticed his uncle's bedroom door was open.

"Where's Uncle George?" Marcus said concerned.

"Your uncle isn't home."

"Huh?" Marcus was immediately disappointed. "What do you mean he's not home?"

Marcus ran into his uncle's room. The bed had been made as if it hadn't been slept in. He returned to the sitting room and sat down on the sofa. He had a pout on his face.

"He was here last night, Momma. He said it would be a while before he had to leave again." Marcus didn't understand.

"Well, son, he had to go. I don't have answers." Rosalia lifted her book up and continued to read. She knew how disappointed Marcus was and felt bad for him. She felt his pain. She also was very upset but didn't want to show it.

Marcus sank further into the sofa. He had hoped to spend some time with his uncle. Now he would have to wait, again.

"How long is he gone for this time?"

Rosalia glanced up and shook her head. Marcus was persistent. She placed the book on the table beside her. "Well, I should be getting your breakfast started so you and Pablo can get your chores done," she said, changing the subject.

chapter

3

IT HAD BEEN A WEEK since George had left the farm. Thankfully, the harvest was almost finished, and Marcus and Pablo would be able to enjoy some time off. They looked forward to it. The boys were in the barn getting the truck ready for the last load of the day, when they noticed the crate in the back of the barn had been moved.

"Hey, Marcus, did you move this crate?" Pablo said.

"Hell, no!"

"Well, I sure didn't!" Pablo said.

Marcus walked over to where Pablo was standing. He looked down at the crate.

"I wonder who moved it?" Pablo said. "Let's move it back."

The boys grabbed opposite corners of the crate and attempted to move it; it wouldn't budge and appeared to be stuck on something.

"What the hell?" Marcus moved backwards and then bent down to investigate. He noticed a rusty metal ring. "Hey, look here." He lifted the ring but nothing happened.

Pablo stood beside Marcus and looked down. "It looks like a handle," he said.

"No shit," Marcus said sarcastically.

"Let's move this thing," Pablo said. The boys dragged the crate a bit more. Pablo started to lift the handle but then he noticed the lock.

"Damn!" Marcus said.

"Look, we better leave it alone and come back another time," Pablo suggested.

Marcus hesitated but eventually agreed.

The boys quickly moved the crate as far over as they could, to where it was when they found it. They had a gut feeling someone was hiding something down there. They jumped back into the truck and drove out of the barn, quicker than their normal speed.

"What do you think is down there?" Marcus said.

"Don't know Marcus, but I wanna find out!" Pablo said excitedly.

As they drove past the house, they noticed someone standing on the back porch; it wasn't their uncle—it was their dad. He must have come home while they were in the barn. Bernardo stared at them as he sucked on the tail end of a Marlboro. He waved to the boys. They timidly waved back at him; they weren't too excited that he was home.

"Do you think he'll ever be the same?" Marcus said, as he reminisced about when their dad used to be home all the time.

"I doubt it, Marcus," Pablo said. "Enough talk. Let's get to work."

Pablo didn't like talking about his dad, because he knew how much it hurt everyone not to have him home. Pablo could feel the distance growing between his dad and the family; he didn't like it.

Rosalia paced slowly back and forth by the back door. She had heard Bernardo's truck pull in. How she longed for him every time he had left. The door suddenly flew open and startled her. Bernardo looked at her. She always seemed to be in the same spot when he arrived home; he knew she missed him. Rosalia ran into his arms before he had a chance to shut the door. He allowed her to cling to him. She put her hands on his rough face and looked into his eyes.

"I missed you so much," she said, as tears streamed down her face.

Bernardo's eyes started to water; he quickly turned his face away. He had to stay strong, or he too would break down. He knew this wouldn't be good for him or his family. He kissed her lips tenderly and then proceeded to push her away. She wanted to hold on. "I need to clean up," he said, as he rubbed her shoulders.

Rosalia wiped her eyes and watched as he walked into the bathroom. He closed the door behind him. She went back to the kitchen. She wanted to sob but held it in. She didn't understand and wasn't sure how much longer she could live like this.

Bernardo emptied his pockets, placed his wallet and cigarettes on the counter, and then stepped out of his heavy boots. His jeans dropped with a *thud* onto the bathroom floor. Once he was in the bath, he didn't want to get out. It felt so relaxing. He closed his eyes and submerged himself into the hot water in the old claw foot tub. After twenty minutes, he thought he had heard a slight knock on the door. He waited for a moment and then rose from the water. He tipped his head to get the water out of his ears. He heard the knock again. "What's up?" he said. There was no answer. "Rosalia?"

"Bernardo, may I come in and take your clothes out to wash?" She was always considerate and asked permission when she needed to do things for him. She had been brought up that way.

"Ummm, sure," he said.

Rosalia slowly opened the door. The relationship between them wasn't like it used to be. There seemed to be a lot of apprehension now, and the intimacy they once enjoyed, was gone. She still wanted him around but knew it would never be the same. She was fearful about their future. Rosalia hurriedly entered the bathroom but refrained from looking at him. She wanted to but knew it would be pointless. She bent down, grabbed his dirty clothes, and rushed back out. Bernardo glanced over but she was already gone. He slid back down into the water. It was hard for him to hold back his emotions.

When George arrived, the parking lot at the clubhouse was empty, aside from the other bikers standing near the back door.

"Hey, Whiskey! Glad you could make it," one of them said.

George turned off his bike and dismounted. He placed his helmet on the sissy bar and then walked towards them. "Hey guys, what's happening?"

"Let's go inside." One of the bikers opened the door and they went in. The door had been unlocked by one of the others, already inside. Boss and Spud were not there. The men entered one of the rooms and closed the door behind them. "Have a seat, George."

George still didn't know the daily routines of the other bikers, or what they did for the club. Since George didn't have many acquaintances in town when he first arrived, he figured this would be the best way to make some, and feel like he belonged to something. George sat down at one of the tables.

"Well, what's going on?" George sat patiently. This was the first time he had been called out to a meeting without Boss and Spud. Boss and Spud were two of the senior members, and usually the ones in command in San Rafael. The names of the two men in the room were: Road Rash and Outcast. They both wore three distinct patches on the back of their vests. George only had two: he had the location patch and the club's name; whereas, the third patch was the club's emblem. This was the important one, so they said. As long as a member who called him out wore the three patches, he was to follow their instructions, without hesitation.

Road Rash looked over at Outcast. He nudged him and whispered, "Are you sure we should be doing this. We aren't even supposed to be in the clubhouse. If Boss finds out, he's going to fucking kill us."

Outcast whispered, "I have it under control." He was also nervous, but tried not to show it. He wasn't pleased that Boss had taken their keys away in the first place. He felt they needed to prove to Boss that they were capable and trustworthy. Boss had no idea the men were doing this. The men sat down across from George.

Outcast took out a piece of paper that had some writing on it. "Okay, just to clarify things, we were instructed to take the last steps in initiating you into the club. If all goes well, you will receive your final patch."

George listened attentively. "Okay, so what do I have to do?"

He wasn't sure if he really wanted to know.

"Here's the address." Outcast passed the paper to George. "You're to be there at 9:00 P.M. You are not to wear your vest, or let on who you are. This is extremely important."

Road Rash watched George's expression.

George nodded. "Who am I meeting?"

"We can't give you any names. The reason for this meeting is for you to find out who the man is in charge of the operation. Do you understand?"

George wasn't sure what this guy was talking about. "What operation?"

"We were instructed not to give you any details. This is where your smarts are going to come in, so that we can be sure you can deal with situations like this on your own." Outcast looked over at Road Rash.

George fidgeted in his seat. "How long is this going to take? I have obligations at the farm."

"That will have to wait," Outcast said.

George thought about what he'd just heard. "Wait. I don't understand."

The bikers realized that George may not have been thoroughly informed as to how serious this club was or how they worked.

"Listen, did you not sign an oath when you joined?" Outcast asked.

"Oath? No ... I don't think so. But, I did sign a piece of paper. I believe it was a membership application. That was over a year ago, so I really don't remember what it said."

"Well, let us refresh your memory," Road Rash said. "The paper you signed was not a membership application, it was an oath. You do know what an oath is?"

George nodded. "Of course I do."

"Well, then you signed the oath ..." There was a brief pause. "Road Rash, go and grab a copy. I believe Whiskey here needs to be refreshed."

Road Rash got up from the table and went to the filing cabinet where they kept the club's documents. It took him a few minutes to find what he was looking for. He pulled out a sheet of paper and passed it to Outcast.

Outcast quickly looked it over to make sure it was the declaration. "Okay, now read this. It might help jar something in that head of yours." He passed it over to George.

George took the paper and read it. "It looks familiar. I've read this before. Where does it say oath?"

Outcast got up from his chair and stood beside George. He pointed to the fine print at the bottom of the page. "Here, read this." He then sat back down.

George moved his eyes down to the bottom of the paper and read:

I, George José Gomez, being a member of Riders of Reason Motorcycle Club, solemnly swear that I will support and honour every member of this motorcycle club when called upon. Each member is to be treated with respect at all times.

Once this oath is signed by the aforementioned, it will be used as a pledge that he understands the significance of it, and the disciplinary actions that will be taken if the family is dishonoured.

The officers of the aforementioned motorcycle club have the right to disclose any of this information to whom they see fit. The officers may also dismiss any member who does not comply with the declaration.

This is a brotherhood, a Family, and the oath binds us to each other, not by blood, but by honour.

George looked up. *Was it too late now to back out?* he wondered. He would lose all the friends he had made if he did, or worse yet, would he even be able to get out? He figured he had better not say anything, or this would make him look foolish. He passed the paper back to Outcast. George looked up as he felt their eyes directed at him. He felt the tension in the room. These men were not fooling around.

"Yes, I read it. No problem," George said.

Road Rash took the paper and filed it back in the drawer.

"Great, now we have that settled," Outcast said.

Rosalia headed out the back door with her arms full of Bernardo's clothes. The washer was down in the basement. Pablo had come up beside her. "Hey, Momma, how are you?" Pablo was the overprotective son.

"I'm okay," she said in a low voice.

Pablo felt she wasn't telling the truth, but he forgave her. He knew how she felt when his dad was home. "It'll be okay, Momma." He put his arm around her and squeezed.

Rosalia nodded her head and leaned on him. "Come on son, your dinner's going to get cold." She closed the basement door and they walked up the back stairs. Marcus was standing on the top stair with a cigarette hanging from his lips. Rosalia didn't approve of the boys smoking but felt nagging at them too much would just make them rebellious.

"You're just like your dad!" Rosalia said and smacked his backside.

Marcus let out a slight chuckle. He knew he was *very much* like his dad. He loved his stepmother, but Marcus knew he wasn't her favourite. Marcus was the black sheep; no matter how hard he tried to impress his parents, Pablo always came out on top. One day he would show them that he was also important. Marcus tossed his cigarette butt onto the dirt below the steps and headed into the farmhouse.

"Smells good, Momma!" Pablo said.

Rosalia smiled and walked over to the stove.

Marcus pulled out a chair and plopped himself down at the table.

"You boys better wash up outside before your dad gets out of the bath," Rosalia said.

Marcus got up and raced his brother out the back door. They cleaned up under the water pump. Marcus cupped his hands full of cold water and tossed it at Pablo, hitting him in the face. Marcus knew this would trigger trouble. He dropped his hands and ran like hell back into the farmhouse. Just as he entered the house, he ran right into his dad.

"Marcus! Damn it! Slow it down!" Bernardo hollered. He aggressively grabbed Marcus and pressed him up against the wall.

Marcus stood there staring at his dad. *What's gotten into him?* he wondered.

Rosalia stopped what she was doing and rushed over. "Bernardo!" she yelled. "What are you doing? Let go of him!"

Bernardo stopped and realized what he had just done. He backed off and apologized to Rosalia and Marcus. "I'm ... sorry. I didn't know ..." He walked over to the table and sat down.

Marcus took a breath and ran back outside. He sat down on the bench and hung his head. Rosalia followed and sat down beside him. She gently put her arm around him. Marcus looked up at her and pushed her away. "I'm fine," he said.

"No you're not, Marcus," she said. "Your dad had no right to act that way with you. He has a lot going on." She disliked having to smooth things over for him when he came home. It wasn't fair to the boys.

"Yeah, I guess," he said. "I wish things were the way they used to be, Momma," he said.

"Me too, son. Come inside and get something to eat. It's getting cold," Rosalia said.

Marcus stood up and went back into the house with Rosalia.

"You boys eat. I'm not hungry," Rosalia said as she placed the casserole dish on the table. She went into the sitting room. Marcus sat beside Pablo and they quietly ate. Bernardo seemed to be in shock. The silence in the room was unbearable. After a few moments, Pablo spoke up. "So, Dad, how was work?"

Bernardo looked up from his plate. "Fine."

"When do you have to go back?" Pablo asked.

"Oh, I'm not sure yet," Bernardo said. "Why?"

"Just curious. I thought you might want to go fishing with us while you're home."

"That would be great," Bernardo said, "if we have time. I noticed the grapes are coming in a bit late this year."

"Yeah, we also had a problem with some of the help showing up, Dad," Pablo said. "But we have it under control."

"Tell you what—if we can get the harvest finished by mid-afternoon tomorrow, maybe then we can go fishing."

A smile crossed Pablo's face. Marcus didn't smile. He was still angry at his dad for pushing him up against the wall. He wanted to hurt him. Marcus had built up frustrations over the years, and they seemed to fester more every time his dad went away and returned.

Marcus spoke finally. "When is Uncle George coming back?" He adored his uncle, because George always listened to him and treated him with respect.

"Not sure," his dad said. "How long has he been gone?" Bernardo glanced over at Rosalia through the doorway, anticipating an answer.

Rosalia noticed Bernardo looking at her, and she shrugged her shoulders. "George was here overnight and then he had to rush off again the next morning. He's been gone for a few days."

Pablo finished his dinner and excused himself from the table. He took his dirty dishes and placed them in the stainless steel sink. He would wash them up later with Marcus. He headed into the sitting room to join his stepmother. She was mesmerized with the flames in the woodstove.

"Momma?" Pablo said, sitting down next to her.

She glanced over at him and placed her hand on his knee, patting it. "I'll be fine." She didn't want the boys to worry about her.

"Momma, how long is Dad going to be working away?"

Rosalia sighed. She had hoped they would find out soon. She didn't want them to know that she had no more of an idea than they did.

There was a sudden *crash* in the kitchen, which made Rosalia jump. "What was that noise?" she called out.

"I dropped my plate on the floor," Marcus said. "Don't worry, I swept it up."

Marcus came out a couple of minutes later.

"Marcus, come sit a moment," she said, as she tapped her free hand on the other side of the sofa. "You boys have been great ...," she said, alternately looking at them.

The boys sat listening to Rosalia. Marcus had lost his biological mother when he was very young and accepted Rosalia as his mother.

"I know this has been tough for both of you," she said, "but hopefully soon, we'll be able to get through all of this and put it behind us."

"What do you mean?" Marcus said. "It's been goin' on for a long time!"

"Shhh, keep your voice down." She placed her finger to her lips.

There was another noise from the kitchen and then Bernardo entered the room. The three of them looked up as though they were hiding something.

"What's going on in here?" Bernardo said gruffly.

"Oh, nothing ...," Rosalia said. She turned her head towards the boys, trying not to look at Bernardo or he would know that she was lying. "How about you boys get the clean-up done in the kitchen, that way you'll be free for the night."

The boys quickly got up from the sofa and went into the kitchen.

Rosalia got up and closed the sitting room door. "Why are you so difficult with the boys, Bernardo?"

Bernardo sat down on the chair next to the woodstove. He glanced over at his wife. His face was tight, as though he were under a great deal of stress. He felt bad. "Things will change soon," he said.

She sat opposite her husband and watched his expressions. "You *know* they are working hard on the farm, and all they want is to spend some time with you. You should be happy they care," she said.

Rosalia got up and left the room. She needed to finish the laundry before it got too late. Bernardo sat staring out of the window. He realized that he had been a bit harsh on Marcus, and that his time away from his family was affecting his mood as well. After a few moments, he got up and went outside.

The boys finished the dishes and headed up to the loft. It was early still. Pablo closed the door and they sat on the edge of his bed.

"What do ya wanna do?" Marcus asked. He was usually full of energy after dinner. Pablo, on the other hand, would rather just curl up and read a book. Pablo shrugged his shoulders. The house was normally quiet and peaceful at night, but with their dad home, they could sense the stress.

Pablo suddenly got up off the bed. "I'm going downstairs to talk to Dad."

Marcus let out a huff and followed him.

They found their dad outside working on one of the trucks. "Need help, Dad?" Pablo jumped up on the front bumper and stuck his head underneath the hood of the truck. "Everything okay with the truck?" Pablo asked.

Bernardo had a flashlight propped between his chin and his chest so he could see down inside where the motor was. He took the flashlight and passed it to Pablo. "Here, hold this." Pablo took it and held it in place for his dad.

"Kinda hard to do everything by yourself, don't ya think?" Pablo said, trying to get his dad to crack a smile.

Marcus felt useless watching the two of them, so he headed off to the backyard to find something else to do.

Just before the sun went down, Bernardo was sitting on the back porch with Rosalia. The boys were out near the barn messing around.

"Don't you boys think it's time to call it a night?" Bernardo hollered out to them. "Four in the morning comes early!"

Rosalia looked over at Bernardo, wishing he would let up on the boys.

"Yes, Dad!" They closed the barn doors and raced to the farmhouse and up the back stairs. Pablo kissed his momma on the forehead, with Marcus tailing behind. They said goodnight to their dad and headed inside.

Rosalia decided she would call it a night as well. Bernardo didn't seem to be very talkative.

chapter

4

ROSALIA WASN'T ABLE TO SLEEP much that night. The old rocker she was sitting on was close to the window. She was careful not to rock it too much because the creaks might disturb Bernardo. She watched silently as he tossed and turned.

Bernardo woke a few times hollering and breaking out in a sweat. She wished she'd known what he was dreaming about. There was more going on with him than he was saying.

She rose from the chair and crept into the kitchen to make some coffee. She picked up the old stainless steel coffee pot and filled it with water, and then dumped some coffee grounds into the percolator and placed it on the stove. She knew the boys appreciated coffee when they woke up. It wouldn't be long now, and the house would come alive with the boisterous voices of maturing teens. The boys hadn't attended school in the last couple of years because of the vineyard responsibilities, and Rosalia wished they could go back and finish. She wanted them to have an education so that they wouldn't have to tend to the farm their whole lives.

Just as the coffee started perking over the top of the pot, the thumping noise of the boys' feet echoed throughout the house as they rushed down the ladder.

"Hey Momma," Pablo said, giving her a hug.

"Morning boys," she said. "Coffee's on, and I've almost finished making your favourites——bacon, eggs and biscuits."

"Dad's not up yet?" Pablo asked, as he sat down nosily at the table.

"No, shhh. He had a rough night," she said quietly, while putting their breakfast on the table.

As though on cue, Bernardo came shuffling into the kitchen with nothing on but his briefs. One could tell he needed to use the bathroom. The boys looked away, as did Rosalia. Bernardo headed into the bathroom. He called out behind him. "Coffee would be great, Rosalia!"

Rosalia, like an obedient wife, poured him a mug of coffee. She set it down and then sat next to Pablo. Bernardo walked out and joined them. He ran his fingers through his tangled hair and let out a grunt. "Well, eat your breakfast boys and get out there."

The boys quickly finished their meal. A few minutes later they got up from the table. They nodded to their mother and headed out the back door. Rosalia closed the door behind them, and then placed their dishes on the counter. She sat back down across from Bernardo.

Bernardo picked up his deck of cigarettes and proceeded to light one. He took a drag and exhaled.

Rosalia couldn't handle the stress anymore. She had to say something.

"How long are we going to live like this, Bernardo?"

He looked up at her. Part of him wasn't there, and he didn't have the answers she needed to hear. It was as if he existed elsewhere. "Not sure," he said. That seemed to be his answer for everything lately.

Rosalia slammed her fist on the table. "Stop saying that, Bernardo! What the hell is going on?" She stood up and stormed over to the open window. She caught her breath and finally said, "You're losing me ... and the boys!"

Bernardo turned to look at her. It wasn't very often she blew up at him, and when she did, it seemed to hit home. "I can't ...," he started to say.

"Can't—can't what?" she asked.

"Can't tell you," he said. He *almost* showed some compassion but then held back.

Rosalia walked over to him and took his hand in hers. "Why, why Bernardo? Why can't you tell me?" The look in her eyes was melting him.

Bernardo got up from the table and walked out of the room. He went into the bedroom, put on some clothes, and then pulled on his boots. He hated coming home, but only because he couldn't say anything to his family. He knew he was losing them, but he didn't have a choice. He wondered if the next time he had to leave, if he should just stay away so that he wouldn't cause anymore harm. It would be a tough decision, a sacrifice, but it would be less stressful. He tossed this over in his head for a bit and then wandered out the back door. He jumped into his truck and tore out of the driveway. He needed to be alone.

Marcus sat on the tailgate of one of the work trucks and stared down the dirt road. He watched as his dad drove away. He didn't know what to do, but like his stepmother, he was getting drained from the bullshit. "Hey Pablo, let's go see what's under that crate!"

"No, we should stay here and get some work done," Marcus said.

"Well, I'm going. I wanna find out what's down there!" Pablo said. He jumped off the tailgate, threw his gloves in the back of the truck and ran towards the barn. Pablo stayed behind for a few seconds, but it wasn't long before he caught up to Marcus. They raced the rest of the way to the barn. Once they were inside, Marcus shut the doors and latched them, so that no one would suspect there was anyone in there. Pablo went over to the crate with Marcus on the other side. The boys pushed and pulled the crate until it uncovered the trapdoor. Marcus lifted the handle.

"We still need a key, Marcus!" Pablo said.

Marcus shook his head. "Damn, I forgot. Is there any other way to get in?"

"Well, let's sweep all the crap off the top and see," Pablo said.

Marcus grabbed an old straw broom, which was in the corner of one of the stalls, and swept the debris off of the trapdoor.

"Okay, stop!" Pablo yelled.

Pablo bent down and noticed that the door had hinges on the other end. "If we can get the hinges off, we should be able to get in," he said.

"How are we gonna do that?" Marcus asked, and tossed the broom on the floor behind him.

The boys sat down on the floor. They weren't sure how they were going to open the door without damaging it.

"Hmmm, let me think," Pablo said. "We could pry 'em out?"

"Maybe we should wait until Dad comes back?" Marcus suggested. "Then we can look for the key while he's home."

"Boy, are you brave!" Pablo said sarcastically.

"Well, what else can we do?" Marcus said.

"We could pick the lock," suggested Pablo.

"Oh, so now you're Sherlock Holmes, are you?" Marcus said, and he snorted devilishly.

Pablo leaned over and slugged him. "Shut-up, asshole! Now let's see if we can find something to pick this damn lock with."

The boys got up and started looking throughout the barn for something they could use.

It was too late. George was involved deeply and there was no turning back. He lowered his head and sniffed the last bit of the white stuff. He felt eyes watching him throughout the room and knew he must not show hesitation. He breathed in deeply and then dropped the rolled piece of paper; it fell on the floor. The cocaine hit him like a ton of bricks as he fell backwards on the sofa, staring vacantly ahead. He had never experienced cocaine in his life and wasn't sure what to expect. Everything was turning into a blur. He had to keep his wits about him and not let on who he was, or what club he belonged to.

George lay on his back. He had no idea where he was. He could barely open his eyes because of the glaring sun. Slowly, he rolled onto his right side. He felt a sharp pain in his ribs. George gritted his teeth from the discomfort, and then rolled over to his other side. *Where am I? Why am I here? What happened?* he wondered. *And where the fuck is my bike?* The last thing he could remember was the room spinning and then everything went black. *Thankfully, I'm still alive*, he thought.

He reached down to his right side. His shirt felt moist, but he wasn't able to put any pressure there. He raised his body upwards onto his elbow, and finally managed to sit up. Looking around all he could see were trees and small hills—no roads. With the back of his hand he wiped the sweat from his forehead. The heat from the sun was blistering. His shirt was saturated in blood. He noticed that his leather vest was gone. *Whoever dumped me here, took that as well. Why?* he wondered. Then he remembered that he wasn't supposed to have worn it in the first place. Suddenly, he was extremely worried. He looked at his shirt more intensely. There was a good-sized rip, and it looked as if it could have been made from the blade of a knife. The blood wasn't gushing so he figured the wound was at least clotting.

George rose to his feet. It was still light out and he figured there was probably two hours before dusk. He hobbled over to a nearby rock and rested against it. Shading his eyes from the sun, he looked around to see if he could figure out where he was. About a mile away, dust was stirring, so he knew there had to be a road. It would take a while to get there, but if he headed in that direction, he may end up on the road sooner than later.

He thought the men at the warehouse must have figured out he was snooping around for information and must have ditched him then. George hoped he hadn't said anything that would jeopardize the *Family*. He wasn't sure what to do, because the others would find out about this and then who knows what the consequences would be; they could be fatal. *Maybe, they would just let me go?* he thought.

Bernardo drove around most of the morning. Around eleven o'clock he pulled into the parking lot in front of the local bar. There were a few vehicles in the lot and some hawgs parked close to the door.

Bernardo climbed out of the truck and walked into the bar. He needed a stiff one to relieve some of the built-up frustrations he was feeling. He hesitantly scanned the bar. There were a few people along one side of the room and some bikers over by the pool table. Bernardo went up to a bar stool and sat down.

"What can I get you?" the bartender asked.

"A double shot of rye," Bernardo said.

"Sure thing." The bartender poured a double shot for Bernardo. He drank it in one swallow, and then set the glass down in front of him. He motioned for another.

"Rough morning?" the bartender asked.

Bernardo nodded and finished off the second drink. He held his hand up as if to say that was enough. The bartender put the bottle down and replaced the cap. "Just let me know when you want another," he said, and wandered away to help another patron.

Bernardo lit up a cigarette and turned slightly on the stool. The bikers were making a bit of a commotion in the corner. Bernardo attempted to hear what they were saying, but he wasn't able to make it out clearly. It was for the better though, because one knows best not to get involved with these types of men. He turned back around and faced the bar. He had an eerie feeling that someone was watching him. A few seconds later, he butted his cigarette out, put a twenty-dollar bill on the counter, and started to head out of the bar. As he opened the door, he briefly glanced back at the bikers.

The bikers turned to each other as Bernardo walked out of the bar.

"Hey man, wasn't that Whiskey's brother?" Road Rash asked.

"Yes, I think it was," Outcast said. "I hope he doesn't know anything."

"I doubt it. I think we've covered our tracks."

"Yeah, but you know what Boss would say if he found out?" said Outcast. "Shit, we already had our keys taken away."

"Fuck Boss! I'm getting tired of his shit. Didn't we do this to prove a point?" said Road Rash.

The bikers were riled up now. The bartender glanced over at

them as if to say 'enough.' He didn't trust them, and didn't want a brawl to break out on his shift.

"Well, I know we'd better keep an eye on this guy, just to make sure he doesn't find out anything," said Road Rash.

The bikers agreed and quickly rose from the table. One of them waved at the bartender on their way out. The bartender was relieved that they were leaving.

Road Rash and Outcast stood outside and watched as Bernardo drove out of the parking lot. They took mental notes of his truck.

chapter

5

IT SEEMED LIKE HOURS before George reached the road. He was in agony and extremely dehydrated. He figured he better sit down and wait for a vehicle to come into sight. He held his side tightly, and looked down to where the wound was. The blood had now hardened on his shirt, so the bleeding must have finally stopped. A few minutes later, he saw a truck heading his way. George needed to flag it down, but wasn't sure if he could get up that quick. He removed his doo-rag and started waving it back and forth; he prayed this would work. He tried to yell, but his throat was so parched there was no use. A sudden rush of hope filled him. *Did the driver see me?* He continued waving his arm. "Come on! Come on!"

There was a sound of gears grinding as the truck got closer to him. It pulled up just ahead of George and then stopped. George was relieved and weak. The driver of the truck jumped out and rushed back to George. "Hey, are you okay?" he asked, as he noticed George holding his side.

"No, I'm not okay." George tried to laugh, but it hurt too much. He took a deep breath. "I need a ride."

"Sure, fella. I can give you a lift. Where ya goin'?"

"Not sure," George said blankly. "I mean—I don't even know where I am."

"Oh, well ... we're just outside of Río Cuarto."

"Río Cuarto?" George said puzzled.

"Yes, you sound surprised?"

"I guess I just haven't scouted these parts before," George said. He really had no clue as to where he was.

"Wow, then how did you get here?"

"Honestly ... I don't know."

"Where's home?" the man asked.

George adjusted himself. The rock he was sitting on wasn't very comfortable. "San Rafael," George said.

"Oh, that's about three hours from where I live. You won't make it back tonight, so you can hang with me at my place. I'll run you into town in the morning."

George thought about it. He didn't know this fellow, but then, he couldn't be as bad as the last ones he had dealt with, could he?

"Here, let me give you a hand," the man said. George grunted while the driver helped him up off the rock. Once George was on his feet, the man helped him up to the passenger side of the truck. "Name's Miguel, yours?"

"George."

"Nice to meet you, George," Miguel said.

Once George was in the truck, Miguel closed the door. The truck was old but in good condition for its age. Inside of the truck smelt of dust and tobacco. There were cigarette butts overflowing the ashtray onto the floor.

Miguel got in and started the truck. It was a standard with three on the column. George hadn't seen a pickup truck like this in a long time. With some hesitation, the truck finally fired up. Miguel put it in gear and off they went.

"How's your side feeling?" Miguel had noticed the blood on George's shirt while he was assisting him into the truck.

"It's quite sore, but I'll be fine," George said, as he continued to hold his side.

"That's quite a wound. What happened?" Miguel asked with concern.

"I'm not sure ..."

"Oh, I see, one of those nights." Miguel had a devilish grin on his face.

George thought he would leave it at that—the less information the better. He wasn't able to give out any about what he was doing or whom he was with anyway.

A good two and a half hours had gone by. George must have passed out. He woke suddenly and straightened himself. It took him a moment before he realized where he was. He looked over at Miguel.

"So, where are we?" George said.

Miguel turned to look at George. "We're on the outskirts of La Costa."

"And how far do you live from here?" George said.

"About another twenty minutes," Miguel said. He reached over with his right hand and banged on the glove compartment. The cover popped open, and while Miguel was reaching for it, the truck started swerved near the edge the road. He pulled out a small flask and loosened the cap with his teeth.

No wonder his teeth looked like that, George thought.

After Miguel removed the cap, he took a big swallow of the hard stuff. "Want some?" He offered the bottle to George. "It might help with your pain."

George got a whiff of it; it was rye. Even though it was George's favourite, he denied.

"Ummm..., no thanks."

"Still sufferin'?" Miguel said sarcastically.

"Yes, sort of." George let out a smirk and turned his face towards the window. He was tempted to wipe the window with his free hand, but thought better of it. He wondered how Miguel could see anything through the filth and smoke stains.

Miguel replaced the cap and tossed the bottle back into the glove compartment. George closed it quickly so it didn't roll out.

"Nothing like a good swig to keep the blood flowing," Miguel chuckled.

George nodded his head. He did his best to be friendly towards Miguel.

Fifteen minutes later, Miguel pulled off the main road and onto a narrower one. The truck barely fit through. George watched intently as Miguel manoeuvred the old vehicle along the meandering road; it was more of a manmade pathway. Miguel sat back in a trance as the truck weaved side to side; it swayed and bounced up and down through the potholes. It was as if the truck knew its way. At the end of the road they stopped in front of a small cottage. The shingles on the roof were tattered, and the outside of the cottage needed repairs badly. The yard needed tending to; it appeared it hadn't been touched in years. Shrubs were overgrown onto the small porch. There was one window in the front and a door.

The inside had to be bigger than it appears on the outside, George thought.

"Well, this is home." Miguel turned the ignition off. "It's not much, but heck it beats sleeping on the ground." He jumped out of the driver's side and closed the door. A moment later, George's door was opened and Miguel offered him a hand out. George held Miguel's arm and hobbled with him up the front steps. Miguel kicked the front door of the cottage open. "Not too many come this way to worry about locking it." Miguel chuckled.

"I guess not," George said. "It is kind of out in the middle of nowhere."

"Just the way I like it," Miguel said.

Once they were inside, Miguel invited George to take a load off his feet and sit on a nearby chair. George felt relieved as he sat down. "How far is San Rafael from here?" George asked.

"Well, depends on which way you go," Miguel said.

"How about the fastest way?" George smiled.

"Oh, about 145 miles," Miguel said. "Be back in a few. I'm gonna run out and get some wood to heat this shack up. Make yourself at home."

"Sure thing," George said, as if he could do much else.

After Miguel left, George stretched out his legs and leaned back in the chair. He pulled his shirt carefully out of his jeans and away from his side. There was an overwhelming sense of heat rushing through him; he winced in pain. He should have just left it alone. He looked down to see if he could see the wound, but it was covered with dried blood, so he wasn't able to. It was quite the gash and it would need stitches. He hoped it would be okay until he made it into town in the morning. *It might be a rough night trying to sleep*, he thought.

Miguel crashed in through the doorway with an armload of wood. A few pieces toppled off the top of the pile and onto the wooden floorboards. They landed with a *thud* and rolled towards the chair George was sitting in. Miguel caught a glimpse out of the corner of his eye at what George was doing. He dropped the rest of the wood down by the woodstove and went over to George.

"Holy shit, man! You have a nasty wound there!"

"Yeah, you could say that," George commented. He was feeling nauseous.

"Let me get you some water and something to clean that up with." Miguel rushed off to the kitchen before George could reply.

George was thankful to Miguel for helping him. Miguel returned promptly with a bowl of warm water and some towels.

"Here, this should help."

"Thank you, Miguel." George sat up a bit and dipped the end of the towel into the water until it was soaked. He then placed it on top of his wound. He felt like he was going to pass out from the excruciating pain. "FUCK!" he yelled, and then fell backwards in the chair.

Miguel took the towel from George's hand and started cleaning the wound for him.

"Sit back. I'll clean it up."

George sat back and closed his eyes. He had never felt this much agony in his life. It took Miguel over twenty minutes before he was satisfied that it was clean enough.

"Do you think it'll be too late to get it stitched up?" George said.

"I think so," Miguel said.

George leaned forward and got his breath. His side was throbbing.

"Like I said, I don't have any plans tomorrow. I'll run you up to

San Rafael," Miguel said. "Then we can get you some medical help."

"You don't have to do that," George said.

"Hey, I don't mind helping out a brother," Miguel said. "That's what we'll do then!" He got up before George could argue with him, and he went over to start a fire. George watched attentively. It was getting late and he would be sleeping in no time, especially after fighting with the pain all day.

chapter

6

"Hey, Marcus! I found something!" Pablo hollered excitedly.

Marcus ran over to his brother. Pablo was holding a small thin piece of wire that had been sticking out of one of the posts of a stall.

"Hmmm that *might* work," Marcus said sarcastically.

The boys went back over to the lock. Pablo bent the wire a bit on one end to make a hook, and then stuck it inside the lock. He had never done this before, but he had seen it done on television.

"Do you know what you're doing?" asked Marcus. He quickly backed away, because whenever he doubted Pablo, he would get slugged in the arm. Pablo would assume Marcus thought he was stupid.

"Ha! Ha! You know better, don't you?" Pablo said, swinging his arm in mid-air but not connecting with anything.

Marcus sat back, laughing hysterically and holding his stomach. He watched his brother continue to fiddle with the wire and lock. Marcus thought it was useless.

"Why don't we see if one of the workers outside knows how to pick a lock?" Marcus suggested.

"Shhh, I can do it!" Pablo yelled. He was getting impatient with Marcus.

The boys weren't having much luck with the lock, and their mother would be wondering where they were soon—especially if she didn't see them out in the field.

"We'd better get back to work," Marcus suggested.

"Yeah, we can try this again later," said Pablo, "when it's dark and no one's up."

The boys pushed the crate back, covering the trapdoor. They headed back out to the field.

Bernardo headed for home. As he neared the farm, he saw the boys working. At least he would be home for a bit to help them out with the last of the harvest. He pulled onto the dirt road that led to their farmhouse. Rosalia was sitting on the front porch looking towards the field. Bernardo could tell she had seen him. She stood up quickly and then ran down the front steps. Bernardo drove the truck into the yard. He stepped out of the truck.

"Bernardo!" she said, flinging herself into his arms. "You left so quickly. I wasn't sure if you were heading back to work." She smelt fresh and clean.

A few seconds later, Bernardo moved back. "I should go help the boys with the rest of the harvest."

"They'll appreciate that," she said. "They've been working so hard, Bernardo."

"Maybe after dinner we'll go fishing down at the Atuel River," Bernardo suggested.

A smile crossed Rosalia's face. She headed back into the house, while Bernardo headed out to the field.

"Dad, over here!" Pablo yelled.

Marcus turned to look. His dad was walking towards them.

"You're back," Marcus said.

"Yes, I'll be home for a couple of days," he told the boys. He tipped the brim of his hat up higher on his head.

The boys were very happy.

"Let's get this harvest in!" their dad said.

They managed to finish the harvest just before dinner. After the boys and Bernardo cleaned up, they rushed inside to be with Rosalia.

She had made breaded veal, sautéed cabbage, sweet rice, and some double-layered biscuits for dessert to celebrate the harvest. They sat down at the wooden table in the kitchen. Rosalia loved seeing them all together. She never knew when the next time would be.

"Sure smells good!" Bernardo commented with appreciation.

The boys dug in; they were starving. They had worked steady for the last three weeks. Another company would complete the wine making, which will be a nice break for the boys. Now they could enjoy some much-needed time off.

"I thought we might go fishing tonight," Bernardo said to the boys.

The boys looked at each other with gleaming smiles. "All right!" they yelled.

Bernardo smiled and nudged Rosalia. "Are you coming?"

Rosalia looked at Bernardo. This was the first time he'd asked her to join them, and she was surprised by the question. "Yes, I would love to!"

"Great! Eat up then—light's a'wastin'!" he said.

As soon as dinner was finished, Bernardo and the boys set off to retrieve the fishing gear from downstairs in the storage area. Rosalia had never gone fishing with them and wasn't sure what to expect. She put on a thick cable knit sweater and made sure she was dressed warm enough for the walk down to the river. It would take at least thirty minutes to get there, and the evenings were cooler—especially by the river. It would be dark in a couple of hours, so they would have to hurry if they wanted to see what they were catching.

Bernardo and the boys came back upstairs and told Rosalia they were ready to go. She followed them down the path towards the river. She had walked here before, but never in the dark. As they got deeper in the woods, the poplar and willow trees towered over them. They reminded Rosalia of giants hovering over their prey, threatening them to leave; it was a creepy feeling. As she thought about it, goose bumps rose on her arms. She often daydreamed and imagined things to be scarier than they actually were. She figured it was from being alone too much. Rosalia walked closer to Bernardo. She grabbed his free hand and tightly squeezed it.

He glanced over at her and laughed. "What's up? You okay?"

"Yes," she said, not admitting to feeling frightened.

"We're almost there," he added.

They walked through the dense woods for a few more minutes before they arrived at the edge of the forest. The daylight was much brighter in the clearing.

The boys had already run ahead to the clearing. Rosalia could hear the rushing water in the distance. The river was rough in the area they were heading, so they would have to hike up the riverbank a ways to where it was calmer, and also so that their lines wouldn't be dragged away. Once they reached the clearing, Bernardo pointed up the river towards an overgrown willow tree that was hanging over the water's edge. "We'll head up that way," he said. The boys were nowhere in sight.

"Where did the boys run off to?" Rosalia asked with concern in her voice.

Bernardo glanced up ahead. "Don't worry, they know where they're going."

The riverbank was quite uneven and rough to walk along, so they took their time so that they wouldn't stumble or fall into the water. It took another five minutes for them to reach the boys. The boys already had their rods ready. Marcus was near a big tree digging for some bait. Bernardo went over to help him. They returned shortly with some big swollen worms. Rosalia sat down on a nearby log and intently watched the boys and Bernardo as they fought with the wiggly bait. They speared them onto the hooks, and in a few moments, their lines were in the water. Rosalia enjoyed being with them. It gave her a peaceful feeling.

Marcus was standing on a large rock in the water, about twenty feet from the riverbank. He cast his line out again and glanced back at his dad.

"Shit!" was all Rosalia heard. Marcus had slipped off the rock and ended up face-first in the cold water. Luckily, the water wasn't too deep. Bernardo could do nothing but laugh at his son. Marcus was soaked, and he didn't find it funny. He was embarrassed. He struggled to get back up on the rock.

"Maybe you should come back here?" suggested Pablo, who was still at the water's edge with Bernardo.

"Shut-up!" Marcus said in a gruff voice. He moved his hand across his forehead to brush away his saturated hair from his eyes.

"Okay boys—enough," Bernardo said. "Marcus, come back here, then you won't fall in again."

Marcus sloshed his way back to where his dad was standing. He stood beside him, shivering.

"Marcus, are you okay?" Rosalia called from the bank.

"Yeah, I'm fine, Momma." Even though he was freezing, he didn't want his mother to baby him in front of his dad.

Rosalia sat back down.

A few minutes later, Pablo hollered, "I got one!"

Bernardo went over to see, and sure enough, Pablo had a big bite. The fish was flipping and flopping in the river. Pablo reeled his line in carefully, then he let the fish run a bit. Once he felt the fish was tired, he yanked his rod and slowly reeled the line the rest of the way in. His dad grabbed the net and tucked it underneath the fish.

"Yes! Look at that baby!" Pablo hollered excitedly.

Rosalia jumped up off the log. "Holy! Nice catch, Pablo!" Marcus stood by in silence. Pablo always caught the fish. Bernardo tossed the fish up onto the riverbank towards Rosalia. She quickly moved away from the fish as it frantically wiggled on the rocks.

"It won't go anywhere." Bernardo chuckled. "We'll have to head back in a few minutes. It's starting to get dark."

Pablo and Bernardo headed out for one more cast before calling it a night. Marcus followed behind them as they crossed the slick rocks. Once they were half-way out, they cast their lines into the river on either side.

"Dad?" Pablo said, while looking up with concern.

"Yes, son?"

"I know you said that we shouldn't ask you about where you work, but ..." Pablo turned his head towards his mother. She was off looking at the different plants that surrounded the embankment and wasn't in hearing distance. "It's just ... I think Momma is having a tough time with you away, especially the last few times."

Bernardo put his free arm around Pablo. He really wanted to tell the boys. *How am I going to do this?* he thought. Bernardo squeezed Pablo's shoulder. "Soon, son, I promise. I will tell you all." He glanced over at Marcus. Marcus was glaring at him. He smiled briefly. He hoped his dad was telling them the truth. They needed to know and so did Rosalia.

"Bernardo!" Rosalia called. "It's getting dark!" There was panic in her voice.

"Yes, dear. We'll be right there," he said calmly. He told the boys that it was time to go. They reeled their lines in. Marcus walked behind them as they got off the rocks.

"Dad, thank you for coming with us, it means a lot," Pablo said.

Bernardo missed this the most—being able to go out on outings with the boys. They were growing so quickly, and soon they would be men and have their own lives.

"Means a lot to me too, son. Hey, it's getting dark fast," Bernardo said quickly, changing the subject. "Pablo, grab your fish and we'll get out of here."

"Yes, Dad, and it'll be even darker when we go back through the forest," Pablo said. "Did you bring a flashlight?"

Bernardo reached into his pocket and pulled out a small one. "Yup, I sure did." He smiled and took Rosalia's hand in his, and the four of them headed to the entrance of the path that would take them back to their farm.

Miguel started the fire, and then he closed the damper. He got up and looked out of the small window. "Yup, it's gonna be a nice day tomorrow. That's quite the sunset over the hills." He pointed out the window to the west. "Are you hungry? I am not the best of cooks, but I am sure I can put something together for you?"

George nodded. He was ready to crash. "No thank you."

"Are you sure? It might make you feel better?" Miguel added.

"No, really, I'm fine. It's been quite the day. I hope tomorrow is better," George said. He let out a big yawn.

"Look, you can sleep on the sofa. That way you won't have to move too far. I'll grab you a blanket. If you need anything else, feel free. My home is your home," Miguel said. "It'll get fairly warm in here in a few minutes. Then it should be good for the night."

George nodded.

"Oh, and the bathroom is just over there beside the kitchen." Miguel disappeared for a moment and returned with an army-grey woollen blanket. "Here you go. I'm going to bed. Sleep tight." Miguel headed off to his bedroom.

George stood up and hobbled over to the sofa. *I sure the hell won't be moving too far tonight*, he thought. He could barely walk as it was. Once he lay down, he leaned back and pulled the blanket up over his legs. He was slightly covered, but at this moment, he didn't care. He closed his eyes and breathed in a deep sigh. He was in pain, but it sure felt good to lie down. Before he knew it, he was fast asleep.

chapter

7

EVERY STEP THROUGH THE FOREST sent shivers up Rosalia's spine. She was afraid of what might jump out at them. Just in case something did, the four of them walked closer together. Bernardo had been through much worse in his time, so he trudged along as though he owned the woods. Rosalia frequently moved her eyes left to right, as if something kept appearing and making her look. She couldn't wait to get out of there. The boys were chuckling behind their parents, and were making unnatural noises off and on, which angered Rosalia. She kept her feelings inside. She didn't want Bernardo to know she was terrified. The walk back felt as if it was an hour longer than it was when they came through earlier. A few moments later, Rosalia could see a glimpse of light through the trees; it was the porch light of the farmhouse. She let out a sigh of relief. The boys hustled ahead of them and raced to the front door. Bernardo and Rosalia took their time getting back. The night air was crisp and the sky was sprinkled with stars. Rosalia shivered and pulled her sweater around herself tighter. Bernardo hadn't said anything yet to Rosalia about having to go back to work again in a couple of days. He would wait until the day he was leaving. He knew if he told her now she would drill him with questions as to where he was going. He didn't need the extra stress, neither did they. "Well, looks like we're going to have fish for breakfast," Bernardo said. "Although, it'll only be a few bites each, seeing as we just caught one." He chuckled.

Rosalia smiled as he opened the front door for her.

He's still a gentleman when he wants to be, she thought.

Mornings were damp and cold in the cottage, so Miguel re-lit the fire. George tossed on the sofa and let out a groan. He couldn't turn over. Miguel heard him and went over to see if he was okay. "George? Are you okay, man?"

George opened his eyes to see Miguel standing over him. "Shit ... I can't move."

Miguel moved the blanket off of George and attempted to look at his wound.

"Easy ...," George said.

"It's inflamed," Miguel said. "You may have a blood clot. We need to get you to San Rafael as soon as possible." Miguel got up and went into the other room. He came back a few minutes later, fully dressed. "We should get going. I know it's early, but it takes a few hours to get there." Miguel helped George sit up and put his boots on.

"I need to clean up a bit, Miguel. Would you mind?"

"No, no, not at all. Just let me know when you're ready."

Miguel helped George to his feet and into the bathroom. He closed the door. "If you need anything, just holler."

"Okay, Miguel," George said.

About twenty minutes later George came out of the bathroom. He didn't look any better than when he went in. He leaned against the wall. He was extremely weak.

"Hey, you should eat something." Miguel grabbed a couple of biscuits and stuffed them in his pocket for the road.

Miguel went over to George and held him up. "I know this is going to be painful, but we have to get you out to the truck, bear with me."

He bent down and let George put his weight on him. George almost collapsed as soon as he stood up. He fell hard against Miguel, but Miguel held onto him. "Okay, this is going to hurt, George, but we have to do it."

He staggered with George towards the front door. George was swearing from the pain and felt sick to his stomach. His free arm went down to hold it, and then his stomach started to heave. Miguel steadied him and waited until George was able to continue. Miguel opened the door with his free hand and helped George the rest of the way down the steps and out to the truck. "Okay, now the tough part is going to be getting you into the truck," Miguel said.

George was out of breath and unable to say anything. He just wanted to sit. They stood by the passenger door for a minute before Miguel instructed George to take in a deep breath. As he did, Miguel used all the strength he had to lift George up to the seat. It was extremely difficult and he almost dropped him. Miguel leaned against him, while George wiggled his way across the seat, until he was sitting properly.

Miguel breathed. "Well, that was a struggle and a half." He laughed. "At least you're in." He reached into his pocket and took out the biscuits. "Here, eat these!"

George still wasn't up to eating, but he took the biscuits anyways. He appreciated all Miguel was doing for him.

"Now let's get out of here!" Miguel shut the door and went back up to the cottage to close the door. He then headed to the truck. He jumped in and started the engine. He glanced over at George. George was as pale as a ghost. "You gonna make it?"

George nodded. He rolled the window down and leaned his head against the edge of the door.

They reached San Rafael just after 8:30 A.M. Miguel parked the truck in the hospital parking lot and ran inside. He returned with a nurse who was pushing a wheelchair. They helped George out of the truck. He was so out of it that he almost fainted.

"He looks rough," the nurse said. "What in God's name happened?"

They helped him into the wheelchair. George wasn't able to talk. He just wanted the pain to end.

"Okay then, let's just get him inside and we'll take it from there," she suggested.

They pushed George into the emergency room where the nurse would examine him. Miguel went back to the waiting room. He didn't want to leave until he found out if George was going to be okay. It was weird; he felt a slight bond with him, and he had no idea why.

The nurse returned about twenty minutes later and asked Miguel to come to the desk.

"Well?" he said.

"It looks like the large gash in his side is infected. I have cleaned it the best I could and have temporarily put in some staples.

"Stitches won't hold now. I don't even know if the staples will hold, or if the skin will heal around them. If we don't get a handle on it right away, the infection could travel elsewhere in his body, if it hasn't already. He is quite feverish.

"He will have to stay here for a couple of days," the nurse said.

Miguel was fidgeting. "I didn't realize he was that bad, or I would have brought him in last night."

"Well, there is no use worrying about that now," she said. "Are you his brother?"

"Ummm, no." Miguel wondered why she would ask such a silly question when he was Mexican and George was Italian. *Do we look alike*, he wondered. "No," he said again, this time more positively.

"He gave me his first name, but I need more information so that I can bill the right insurance company," she added.

"I don't know his last name," Miguel said.

"Oh?" the nurse said.

"Actually, I just met him last night on the side of the road. He never said what happened to him and I didn't pursue it," Miguel said.

"I guess I will have to ask him some more questions then," she said.

"So, is he gonna be all right?" he asked.

"Yes, let's hope so," she said. "Did you want to see him?"

"Yes," Miguel said.

The nurse led him down the hallway to where George was. "I'll leave you two alone for a few minutes," she said as she closed the door behind him.

George was settled more now and staring towards the window.

"Hey buddy, how you doin'?" Miguel strolled over to the side of the bed.

George turned to look at him. He had been medicated, so he was quite groggy and feeling no pain. "Good ... now." He displayed a shit-eating grin.

"Great! Look, I'm ... gonna have to run," Miguel said. "I hate having to leave you like this. Is there anything I can do, or anyone I can call?"

George thought for a moment. "Yes. Could you give the nurse my brother's number, so she can let him know that I'm here?"

"Sure, not a problem." Miguel hunted down a pen and some paper. He came back and handed them to George.

George took them and wrote on the paper. "My brother's name is Bernardo Gomez and I've written his phone number on here. He should be home, I think. If not, tell the nurse she can leave a message with his wife, Rosalia." George handed the pen and paper back to Miguel.

"Great. I can do that. And hey, if you're ever down this way again, don't be a stranger!" Miguel put his hand out to George's.

George shook his hand with a firm grip, the best he could muster in the condition he was in. "Thanks for everything. I owe ya."

"Not a problem, Bud." Miguel headed out of the room.

The nurse returned moments after Miguel had left. "So, Mr. Gomez ..."

George smiled. She was the prettiest thing he had seen in quite some time. Then when you're around gruff belligerent bikers all the time, any female is a welcome sight. She was about five-foot-five with short auburn hair. She was cute; her figure was petite. He could crush her in no time, if he so desired, or other things. As his mind wandered, he smiled. The lust was clearly apparent in his eyes and groin. "Yes," he responded after a bit of daydreaming. The medication was definitely working.

"I'll call your brother momentarily to let him know how you're doing. I noticed you didn't have any ID on you. Do you know what your medical insurance number is?" The nurse sat on the edge of the bed. Her legs crossed and revealed how toned and sleek they were.

George couldn't help but move his eyes from the bottom of her ankles to where the hem of her skirt ended. "I don't know it off hand, but Bernardo might know." There was a brief pause before George realized what the nurse had just said.

"What do you mean I didn't have ID? It should have been in my wallet?" George was suddenly confused.

"No, George. There was nothing in your jeans, not even a wallet."

Damn, he thought, *they must have taken that too when they dumped me in the middle of nowhere.* "Shit ... I mean ... errr, damn. Look, is there any way I can talk to Bernardo? I mean, it would be better, and he won't worry as much if he heard from me."

"Well, you shouldn't move yet," said the nurse. "If we wait a few more hours, then maybe I can wheel you out to the phone to call him."

"Okay, you can wait that long for the information?"

"Yes, I guess I'll have to," she said. "Listen, I need you well-rested for tomorrow, because we'll have to discuss what happened to you."

George nodded. *How am I going to explain anything to her when I can't remember?* he thought.

George had dozed off and on during the day because of the medication. Andrea, the nurse, was unable to wait any longer to contact George's brother. She went out to her station and picked up the phone. She dialled Bernardo's number. She sat down in a nearby chair and waited.

The phone rang three times before someone answered.

"Hello?"

"Hi, this is Andrea Walters. I'm a nurse and I'm calling from the hospital. May I speak with Bernardo Gomez?"

"This is Bernardo."

"Great. Listen, George Gomez, your brother was admitted to emergency this ..."

"George? Is he okay?" Bernardo asked, cutting her off.

"Oh, yes, he's okay, but we need to keep him in for observation."

"What's wrong? What happened?" asked Bernardo.

Rosalia was in the sitting room when she'd overheard part of the conversation. She rushed in and stood beside Bernardo.

"He has an injury in his side—a big gash. I'm not sure what happened. I'm hoping George will be able to give me more information tomorrow."

"Can I see him?"

Suddenly, Rosalia was very concerned. *George was hurt? How? Where was he?* She kept quiet and listened while Bernardo talked.

"Yes, you can come in to see him for a few minutes. Oh, and the reason I'm calling is because I need the name of his insurance company so that we can complete the paperwork."

"I believe George has that information in his wallet," Bernardo said.

"Well, that's the problem," the nurse said. "He's lost his wallet, so he has no identification or other documents to verify anything."

"Well, that's not good. Listen, he deals with the same company I do. I'll bring the contact information with me."

"Please remember, you may come in anytime until 9:00 P.M.," she said. "Then we close the doors for the night, unless there's an emergency."

"Great. I'll be up there in twenty minutes." Bernardo hung up the receiver.

Rosalia looked at Bernardo. "Is George okay?"

"Yes," Bernardo said.

"Was he in a motorcycle accident?"

"No ... actually, I'm not sure. The nurse couldn't give me much information, because George hasn't told her anything. I'm going to go up and see him."

Rosalia's shoulders slouched. She wanted to go with him. *Why isn't he asking me to join him?* she wondered. She took in a deep breath ... "Bernardo, may I come with you?"

Bernardo turned towards her. "Not this time. George is ... he's incoherent right now and the nurse needs information regarding his medical coverage. It's dark out, and I want you to stay here with the boys. I promise. I won't be long."

"But Bernardo ... are you sure ... I would like to see him," Rosalia begged.

Bernardo felt something odd about the way Rosalia was concerned about George all of a sudden. He bent down and gave her a kiss. He held her close for a moment. Rosalia was a bit hesitant. He kissed her again, this time with more intensity.

Rosalia smiled. His passion was unexpected and seemed to temporarily snap her out of her thoughts about George. "Okay, Bernardo. I'll be waiting for you."

Bernardo grabbed his jacket and truck keys, waved to her from the front door, and then ran down the steps. Within minutes, he was on his way to the hospital.

chapter

8

Boss was feeling much more at ease now that they had sold the drugs. He disliked having to keep them at the clubhouse too long. The deal went smoothly. Boss and Spud were sitting in the meeting room having a beer when one of their members walked in.

"Hey guys." The biker had a vest in his hand. "I found this over by one of the bins outside, and thought I outta bring it to you."

Boss got up from his chair and took the vest. He turned it over. The nametag 'Whiskey' was on the back of it.

"That's odd." Boss noticed that all the club patches had been ripped off. "We need to have a meeting, Spud. Get a hold of the rest of the members. We'll meet tonight."

Bernardo arrived at the hospital twenty-five minutes later. He rang the buzzer on the outside wall, and an elderly woman opened the door. "Yes, may I help you?" she said.

"I'm Bernardo. I'm here to see George Gomez."

"Come in." She closed the door behind them and went to check the list of patients. "We're almost closed for the night, but you're welcome to visit for a few minutes."

She led Bernardo down a hallway towards George's room. There was a nurse in the room with him. "Bernardo?" the woman in the room said.

"Yes," he said.

"Great! I'm Andrea," she said. "I've been taking care of George since he arrived."

Bernardo looked at George. He was asleep. The nurse led Bernardo out to the other room to talk to him.

"George has been in a lot of pain today," she said. "We were finally able to sedate him so he could get some rest. Did you bring the insurance information?"

Bernardo reached into his back pocket and pulled out his wallet. He flipped through it and pulled out his medical card. "Here you go," he said. "George uses the same company, but you'll have to contact them to get his number."

"Thank you, Mr. Gomez," she said.

She took the card and went over to her desk. She wrote down the information and then returned it to Bernardo. She pointed to the chair on the other side of the desk. "Have a seat."

"Sure, thank you," Bernardo said. He sat down across from her.

"We need to know what happened to George," she said.

Bernardo wasn't sure what to tell her. "I don't know, Miss. I haven't seen George for over a month."

The nurse looked at him. "Okay. I'll let you see George for a few minutes. We're going to keep him for another day, so that I can make sure the infection hasn't spread."

Bernardo nodded, got up, and followed the nurse back to George's room. "He sure doesn't look well," he said.

"Well, he's lost a lot of blood, and the infection has taken quite a toll on him," she said.

"I guess he's lucky to be alive," he said.

"Yes, very lucky," she added.

"How did he get here?" asked Bernardo.

"A man brought him in," she said.

"Who?" Bernardo asked.

"He said his name was Miguel, but that was all," she said. "Miguel said he picked George up on the side of a road."

"I see, so that doesn't really answer any questions," he

commented.

"No, it doesn't," she added. "I'll leave you two alone for a few minutes. Please don't wake him."

The nurse left the room and closed the door behind her. Bernardo sat on the chair beside the bed and stared at George. He was thankful at least that George was alive. He really wanted to know what had happened to him. He sat there for another ten minutes hoping that George would wake up, but he hadn't. The nurse returned and escorted Bernardo out of the hospital. "I'll give you a call when George will be discharged," she said.

Bernardo shook her hand. "Thank you for everything."

He headed back home.

While Bernardo was driving home, he couldn't help think back to how Rosalia was acting. *Was he really losing her?* he wondered.

After the meeting that night, Boss and Spud weren't impressed that someone would send Whiskey out on his own. It was against the club's rules. Anything the club did, they did in pairs—not alone. Another member at the meeting revealed that George had been admitted to the local hospital and would be released in a few days. No one would snitch as to who sent George out in the first place.

"Spud, we need to get to the hospital before anyone else. Maybe Whiskey will tell us what happened and who sent him out," Boss said.

"I still can't believe that no one is stepping up," Spud said.

"The only thing we can do is question Whiskey and hope he tells us," Boss said.

"And what if we don't get answers?" Spud said.

"Well, we'll take that as it comes," Boss said. "Get me a phone book and I'll call the hospital."

Spud rummaged through a drawer for the phone book. He passed it over to Boss.

"Punch in the number and pass me the phone," Boss said. He sat back in his chair waiting.

Spud entered in the number and then gave Boss the receiver.

Boss waited for someone to answer.

"Emergency, Lauretta speaking. How can I help you?"

"Hello, Ms. Lauretta. I am hoping you can help me. I'm looking for a man who was admitted a few days ago; his name is George Gomez."

"Oh, George, yes he's here. We have him on the upper floor. Let me check his chart. I will be right back," she said. She was quite pleasant on the phone.

A moment later she came on the line and said, "Yes. He is here."

Boss shook his head, she just said that. "Thank you, Miss. I am calling to see what time he is being discharged."

"Hmmm, it looks ... let's see, today's Sunday ... oh yes, Wednesday at 10:00 he is being released. Is there anything else I can help you with?"

Boss chuckled to himself. She wasn't too bright. "No, no thank you. That's all I need to know."

"Who may I ask is calling?" she asked.

The line went dead.

"That's odd," she said. She hung up the receiver and didn't think any more of it.

"Okay Spud, we'll be heading to the hospital Wednesday morning," Boss said.

"Great. Do you think it's a good idea?" Spud asked.

"Sure, why not? Let's call it a night."

Boss locked the clubhouse on their way out.

When Bernardo arrived home the lights were all out. He assumed Rosalia had turned in for the night. He felt bad that he hadn't spent much time with her. He closed the front door quietly and kicked off his boots. The house was very peaceful.

He walked into the bedroom and found Rosalia sitting on the edge of the bed. Her head was down as though she was reading. Bernardo knocked lightly on the door so that he wouldn't startle her. She lifted her head and then got up to meet him.

"Are you okay?" he asked.

"Sure," she said. She rubbed her eyes. She had been crying but didn't want Bernardo to know.

Bernardo gave her a hug and held her for a moment. He felt like there was something wrong. He lifted her chin and looked into her eyes. "Are you sure everything's okay?"

Rosalia didn't want to discuss what was going on. She knew it would upset him. She was very worried about George and didn't want Bernardo to know. Bernardo was jealous at times and this wouldn't be the right time for it. "Yes, I'm fine. How's George doing?" she asked.

"He's doing well. They said they would be discharging him soon. I wasn't able to talk to him because he was sleeping," he said. "He looks a bit banged up but not near as bad as I'd expected." He lied so it wouldn't alarm her.

Rosalia turned away and said, "That's great, Bernardo. Listen, do you mind if I turn in? I'm really exhausted."

"Me too," he said. "It's been a long day."

Rosalia loved her husband more than she had loved anyone in her life; however, she was slipping away. More than anything, she wanted to rekindle their love, but she knew, deep down, it would never come back. Her heart hurt and she was feeling lonely.

George woke up to a nurse taking his pulse. He rubbed his eyes a bit with his free hand. She wasn't the same nurse from the previous night.

"Morning, sleepy head," she said. "You slept through the whole night. How do you feel?"

George flinched. The pain was still intense. "It's very sore."

The nurse let go of his arm. "Can you turn over?" she asked.

George tried to turn a bit. "Yes, but just barely."

"Well, at least you can move, and that's a good sign," she said. "I think a couple of more days, and then we can send you home."

George looked up at her. "Has someone talked to Bernardo?"

"Yes, apparently he was in last night for a bit. You were asleep though," she said. "He brought us your insurance information."

"Great," he said. "Did he say anything else?"

"No, not that I know of," she said. "Are you sure you're okay, George?"

"Oh ... uhhh, yes," he said, as he winced in pain while adjusting his posture.

"How did you get that gash in your side?" she asked, hoping he would remember something.

"I don't know."

"Was there anyone else was with you?"

Oh gawd, George thought. *Think! Think!* "You know, I wish I could remember, but ..."

"Were you unconscious at all?"

George felt like the nurse was interrogating him. He preferred the nurse on duty last night over this one; she seemed to be more understanding and sympathetic. "Yes, I think the shock made me pass out." He figured he may as well say something, even though he really didn't know if he had passed out or not, but this way she might stop questioning him.

"I see. So you don't remember who you were with?" There was a pause. "Would your brother know?"

"I'm not sure. You would have to ask him." George was getting irritated.

The nurse felt his attitude change and decided to leave it at that for now. She walked over to the side of his bed and pulled the sheet down without warning. George tried to grab it but it was already off.

"We need to see how your wound is doing," she said.

George pushed himself higher on the bed with his elbows, and braced himself; he had a feeling this was going to hurt.

The swollen gash in his side didn't look healthy.

"We are going to have to take you in," she said, and she covered him back up.

"What do you mean, take me in?" He was confused. She wasn't the best one for explaining things; she said things so bluntly that one would have to read her mind before you could understand what the hell she just said.

"To operate ... clean your wound out. Sorry for the confusion."

"When?" George asked.

"Soon, I will need to make some calls and get some staff in here.

This is a very small hospital, and we don't have the personnel on hand. I'll be back in a little while." She picked up his chart and made some notes on it. "We won't be able to feed you until afterwards, because it might make you sick." She patted George on the hand and then left. He hated that. He felt like she was mothering him.

As she opened the door, he made a scrunched-up face behind her back; he disliked her. If he could get up on his own, he would be gone. He sat there thinking for a bit. *I wonder if Bernardo will come and pick me up?* It was early yet, and he figured Bernardo would be home. He decided against it. He lay back on his pillow and closed his eyes.

chapter

9

AN HOUR LATER, the nurse returned with a couple of interns. They prepped George for surgery and hooked him up to an intravenous. In seconds all was dark.

The surgery was over within the hour and George awoke just after 2:00 P.M. His mid-section was wrapped in bandages. He rubbed his eyes until he could see clearly.

There was another nurse in the room folding some sheets. She glanced over at George as he tossed in the bed. "How are you doing?" She placed the sheet on a shelf and walked over to the side of his bed.

"Okay, I think. How did it go?" he asked.

"Well, I think they got it all. They removed the staples, cleaned the wound, and then stapled it up a lot tighter than it was. It looks like you'll live." She wandered back over to the pile of sheets she was folding and continued. Her nametag read 'Bernice.' She was a heavy-set girl, with red wavy hair down to her shoulders. Her figure was hidden by the loose scrubs she was wearing, but he could tell her breast size had to be at least a 'D.' She wasn't the most attractive woman he had ever seen, but she wasn't hard to look at either.

"So, when's lunch?" George asked, trying to clear his thoughts and focus on his stomach instead.

"Oh? So you're feeling better then?" she said. "Just a moment,

I'll see what I can get for you." She went out to find George something to eat.

A few minutes later, Bernice came in carrying a tray. She set it on the table in front of George. "It's not hot, but at least it's something." She lifted the cover off the plate. "Look at this feast!"

George peeked over the tray. "Good gawd, you call this a feast?"

Bernice elevated his bed. "Well, yes. If you'd lived on the streets you would." She smiled, and went back to folding the sheets.

George shook his head. *She sure had a way with words, and she thinks she's humorous?* She was in a way, but George sure didn't want to admit it. He sat up the best he could and tried to stir up an appetite for what sat in front of him.

Ugh. He hoped dinner was going to be better. George picked up what they called a sandwich and took a small bite. There was no butter on it, no salt, nothing but a piece of ham. It was worse than prison food. He tried chewing it but it was almost impossible. He reached for the coffee that was there. He took a sip. "Ack!" It was instant and cold. "What the fuck?" George pushed the tray away. "How can you feed this to sick people?"

Bernice came back over to his bedside. "Is it cold?"

"Yes," George said in a slightly gruff voice.

She could tell that he was extremely disgusted. "I guess the warmer must have been turned off."

"Really? No shit ..." George replied sarcastically.

"Look, I tell you what. I'm going to sneak out and get you some real food," she told him.

George looked at her. "Why would you do that?"

"Well, because I agree. This stuff is shit," she said. "Give me about thirty minutes and I'll be back."

George thought that was very sweet of her. She didn't have to do that. He smiled and nodded appreciatively.

Bernice took the tray and dumped the contents into the garbage can and then left the room.

George sat back in his bed. He was already tired of being in the hospital, and hoped it wouldn't be much longer. He closed his eyes for a few moments.

Bernice returned within a half hour with some hot food from a fast food restaurant down the street. George was very grateful. It didn't take him long to devour all of it. He was now full enough to have a good sleep.

Bernice came in a few minutes later to give him some more medication. He wasn't feeling any pain. He nodded off until late in the afternoon.

Morning had arrived sooner than Rosalia wanted. Bernardo had tried to hold her all night, but every time he attempted she would nudge him away.

The morning dragged by slowly as Rosalia thought about her life and what the future may hold. While she was preparing breakfast, Bernardo came up behind her and pulled her close to him. She felt his warm breath on her neck. He was trying so hard to show his love for her, but maybe he had waited too long.

Pablo wandered in shortly after, and spotted them in the corner in a deep embrace. For his momma's sake, he liked to see this. "Excuse me," he said, as he cleared his throat.

Bernardo looked his way and slowly moved back from Rosalia. "Son, what's up?"

"Are you home for a while?" Pablo asked abruptly.

Bernardo looked over at Rosalia. He wasn't able to lie in front of them both. "Well, son, I do have to go to work this morning."

Rosalia quickly looked at him, in shock. She didn't realize he was heading out so soon, just when she was beginning to think he was starting to relax.

Bernardo tried to change the subject. "Your uncle will be staying for a while." He hoped this would add some comfort. "George won't be going anywhere for some time."

"Uncle George? Where is he?" Pablo asked.

Bernardo wasn't sure how to break the news to Pablo about his uncle being in the hospital. He had to think of something to tell him so he wouldn't be too alarmed. But at the same time Bernardo couldn't lie to him. "He's at the hospital, son."

"Hospital? What's wrong?" Pablo asked.

"We're not exactly sure, but he should be home soon," Bernardo said. "You can ask him when he gets here."

"Okay," Pablo said, "but why do you have to go so soon?"

"I hope to be back in a day or two," Bernardo said. He turned to Rosalia and gave her a quick kiss. On his way out of the kitchen, he turned his head and said, "See you all soon." Rosalia just stood there, appalled.

Marcus had overheard them talking and rushed into the room.

"Leaving again?" Marcus said sternly.

"Yup," Bernardo said. "See you in a day or two, son."

That was the end of the conversation before they heard the truck fire up and take off out of the driveway.

There was silence in the house the rest of the morning.

"Well boys, I need to lay down for a while," Rosalia said. "Would you mind?"

"We don't mind," Pablo said. It was odd for their Momma to take a rest so early in the morning.

"Don't forget there are chores that need to be tended to," she added.

The boys nodded and off they went out the back door.

"Pablo, do you think Uncle George is okay?" Marcus asked.

Pablo shuffled his feet through the loose dirt on their way to the barn. "I don't know, but I sure wish Dad would fucking stay home!" Marcus felt the same way.

The boys entered the barn and closed the door behind them.

"Let's figure out what the hell is down there!" Marcus hollered excitedly. He propped some wood against the door.

Pablo was over by the crate and waited for Marcus to help him move it aside. He also wanted to find out, once and for all. Once the crate was moved, the boys pried the hinges off the edge of the trapdoor with a nearby shovel.

"Oh shit!" Marcus quickly backed away from the trapdoor. The end of the trapdoor, where the boys removed the hinges, had suddenly fallen through the floor!

"I think we got it open," Pablo said sarcastically.

Marcus chuckled. Except now, it would be very difficult to make it look like they hadn't been down there. The boys got down on their knees and looked through the opening. "It's dark down there! We'll have to crawl down the door."

"Do we have a light?" Pablo said. He scanned the barn for something, but didn't see anything.

"We need a light before we can go down there," Marcus added. "I can't see a damned thing!"

"Yes, I know, Marcus. Let me think." Pablo looked down into the dark hole again. He spotted something shiny on the wall, but he wasn't sure what it was. "I'm going down," he said. "You keep an eye out."

"Okay, but don't be long," Marcus said in a panicked voice.

Pablo waddled down the door on his ass until his feet hit bottom. He waited for a moment until his eyes adjusted a bit to the darkness. He then looked to where he saw the shiny object. He moved his hand around in the dark carefully so as not to bump against anything. He felt the object. It was hard, smooth, like glass. He wrapped his fingers around it and carefully pulled on it. It wasn't budging, so he lifted it gently. The object let go and he raised it up out of the hole, so they could see what it was. "Here Marcus, we've lucked out. It's a lantern!"

Marcus grabbed onto it.

"Hey, now we only need some matches," Marcus said. "Do you have any?"

Pablo reached into his shirt and pulled out a box of matches. "Here you go!" He tossed the box up to Marcus.

Marcus picked the box up off the floor and attempted to light the lantern, but it wasn't working. "It won't light, Pablo!"

"Try pumping it first, dumb ass!" Pablo hollered.

Marcus found the small lever on the side of the lantern and pulled on it. He then pushed it in and out a couple of times. He struck another match and finally it lit. "Got it!" Marcus yelled excitedly. I'm coming down," Marcus said.

"No, not yet," Pablo said. "Pass me the lantern first, so you don't drop it. The door is very slippery."

"Okay Pablo." He passed the lantern carefully down to him.

Once Pablo got it, he turned the dial to minimize the flame. Marcus started to go down the trapdoor. He slid partway before he suddenly stopped.

"Come on Marcus, just a little more," Pablo said.

Marcus managed to slide the rest of the way without running Pablo over. Once down, he stood beside Pablo. Pablo put the lantern on the ledge. The enclosed area had been there for quite some time and was well-built. They figured it must have been a storm shelter at one time. The boys were in awe as they scoped it out.

"Wow, Pablo, and to think we didn't know this was here!"

Pablo walked around the small area. There weren't that many cobwebs, so the boys knew someone was down there not too long ago.

"Who do you think comes down here?" Marcus asked.

"I'm not sure," Pablo said.

Marcus got a shiver down his spine; he was nervous. "What if Dad finds out we were here, Pablo? What do you think he would do?"

Pablo tried not to think of the consequences. They hadn't seen anything that would get them into trouble ... yet.

George slept deeply because of the medication, and woke around 7:00 P.M. He had a feeling he'd missed dinner. *No, not again,* he thought. He couldn't handle another meal like the one he had earlier, and he figured Bernice would be gone for the day. He rang the buzzer that was hanging on the edge of his bed. It took a couple of rings before a nurse came in. It was Bernice. *She must be working overtime,* he thought.

"Did I miss dinner?" he asked.

Bernice came over to the side of the bed and took his pulse. "Just a moment." After she was done, she said, "Yes, you missed it. If you give me a minute, I'll get you some."

"I think I'll pass," George said. "I'm ... not hungry."

"Well, you need to eat to keep your strength up. I hear they are discharging you in the morning, but if you're not eating they will keep you in longer. I have instructions to call your brother to discuss details for your recovery, and to find out who's picking you up."

"Oh? That quickly?"

"Yes, if patients don't have life-threatening wounds, we don't keep them in too long."

"I see, what if there isn't anyone to help me out?"

"Isn't there?"

"Well, I can't just assume Bernardo and his wife will help me, can I?"

"Is that your residence?"

"Well, yes, for now."

"Then we have no choice but to send you there. I'll be right back with your dinner."

George figured Bernice was tired, because she didn't seem as friendly as she did earlier. *The long hours can take their toll on nurses*, he thought.

Rosalia had laid down for about an hour and wasn't able to sleep. She decided to get up and try to keep herself busy. She went into the kitchen to tidy up.

Suddenly, the phone rang and startled her. She almost dropped the plate she was drying. She placed it carefully back in the dish rack, dried her hands on her apron, and then reached for the receiver. "Hello?"

"Hello, this is Bernice, a nurse at the hospital. Is Bernardo there?"

"No. He's gone for a bit," Rosalia said. "He's been called away to work."

"I'm calling to make arrangements for someone to pick George up tomorrow," Bernice said.

"Well, I'm not sure when he'll be back," Rosalia said. "How is George doing?"

"He's doing well. He had a minor operation, but it all seems to have gone well, and we'll have him up on his feet tonight. We have had him sedated and confined to the bed since he arrived, but I think he'll be fine with a little care. He'll have to take it easy for a while." There was silence on the line. "So, you don't know when you expect Bernardo?"

"No, miss."

"Is there any way you would be able to pick George up?"

Rosalia thought for a moment. "I could get Pablo to drive in and pick him up. Pablo's his nephew."

"That'll work. Can you have him come in around ten tomorrow morning?" the nurse asked.

"Yes, I'll let him know tonight. He doesn't have any other plans, except for around the farm."

"Great. We'll see Pablo in the morning. Have a good night."

Rosalia replaced the receiver. The boys were outside doing their chores. Even though the harvest was finished, there were still the daily chores that needed to be done so their momma wouldn't be overworked. Rosalia would talk to the boys later that night.

chapter

10

P̲ABLO BUMPED into a wooden box.

"Marcus, come here!"

Marcus walked over to where Pablo was. It was very cold where they were, and there were a lot of creaking noises, which gave Marcus the willies.

"Should we open it?" Pablo said.

Marcus looked at him. He could sense Pablo was nervous, and it usually took quite a bit to get him that way.

"Well ...," Marcus started, "I think we're in trouble now, so why not?"

Pablo looked at his brother. Neither of them liked being this secretive towards their dad, and this might ruin their relationship with him, but they had to take a chance. Both were also tired of trying to please him, when he never showed respect for them or their momma. The boys pondered for a few minutes on whether or not they should do it.

"Okay, Marcus. Let's do it!" Pablo said. He jumped off the wooden box they had been sitting on.

Suddenly the boys heard a noise above them. "What was that?" Marcus said.

"I'm not sure," Pablo said. "You go up and check." Marcus gave him a dirty look. *Why do I have to always do the shit jobs*, he thought to himself. He knew better than to argue with Pablo right now, because whoever was up in the barn would hear the commotion.

Marcus turned and started to go up the fallen trapdoor. It was a bit more difficult going up. It took him a couple of times before he managed to get a grip with his feet. He was more careful this time because he already had a couple of slivers from slipping down the boards. Once he was near the top, he slowly looked side to side, but didn't see anyone. He got up out of the hole and ran to the front of the barn to make sure there was no one out there. *So far, so good*, he thought. Marcus jogged to the hole in the floor and carelessly slid back down.

"You should be careful. You might get slivers elsewhere!" Pablo laughed, although it would surely hurt if it had happened. Then Marcus would have some explaining to do.

"Okay, let's see what's in this box," Pablo said. Marcus lifted one end of the box while Pablo lifted the other end. Together they managed to lift it enough to see inside. Pablo reached for a piece of wood to prop it open.

"Get me the lantern, Marcus!"

Marcus let go of his end and the top managed to stay open, but then it started to droop on one side.

"Hurry!" Pablo yelled.

Marcus came back with the lantern and shone it towards the inside of the box. Pablo reached in and pulled out something; it was a book. He carefully brushed the dust off the cover. The book was aged. The letters had been embossed with silver but most of them had been worn off from being stored; however, the boys were still able to read the title from the imprints. Pablo traced the letters slowly with the index finger of his right hand as he read the words: "R—i—d—e—r—s ... o—f ... R—e—a—s—o—n."

The cover was made of fabric; it used to be jet-black in colour. The fabric wrapped around the front, spine and the back of the book. It was now very scuffed up and a dingy black and grey colour.

Pablo opened the front cover. As he opened it, he felt the spine crack. It had been sitting in the box for quite some time. The inside pages were yellowed and the edges were extremely ratted.

Marcus moved closer to Pablo, showing great interest in what they had found. "Wow, Pab! This book is old!"

Pablo nodded as he carefully thumbed through the pages.

"How long do you think it's been down here?" Marcus asked. It was very hard for him to control himself. It was as if they had found the biggest treasure ever.

Pablo hushed Marcus. "Look Marcus, I know this book is old, but we have no idea whose it is."

"What does it mean?" Marcus asked.

"I'm not sure." Pablo thumbed through the book. There were plenty of pictures of bikers—hard-ass bikers and hundreds of them. He flipped to the front of the book and started reading. He looked up at Marcus. "Marcus, ... this book seems as though it's from a motorcycle club called 'Riders of Reason,' and by the looks of it, it's not a friendly club. I think we should take this book inside. I want to read it!"

Pablo placed the book down on the floor beside him and reached into the box again. He found a bottle and pulled it out. "Whiskey?"

"Let's try it!" Marcus said. Pablo wasn't so sure. He had seen drunken men before, and he didn't know if he liked what it did to them.

"No, we'd better not," Pablo said. "We'll be caught for sure." Pablo carefully placed the bottle back inside. They came across more papers regarding the motorcycle club, as well as immigration papers, passports and other paraphernalia.

"Do you think this is Uncle George's stuff?" Marcus asked.

"I'm not sure." Pablo didn't want to think that his uncle was involved in a motorcycle gang. He wondered whose stuff it could be if it wasn't their uncle's, because their dad didn't own a motorcycle. "Look," Pablo said, and passed Marcus some of the papers and a passport.

Marcus looked them over, but he didn't recognize any names. "This is weird, Pablo?"

"No kidding. I think we should find out whose stuff it is," Pablo said.

"So, now what?" Marcus plunked himself down on the dirt floor.

"Whoever owns it, is going to kill us if they find out we know anything."

"Marcus, don't be silly," Pablo glanced down at his watch. "We need to get out of here. It's after 3:00!"

Marcus quickly got back on his feet.

Pablo headed up the trapdoor with the book tucked under his arm. While he was doing that, Marcus reached into the box and pulled out the bottle of whiskey. He quickly stuffed it into the back of his jeans. He pulled his shirttail out to cover it. Pablo went back down and helped Marcus close the lid. They positioned it the best they could so that it looked like it hadn't been opened.

"How are we going to shut the trapdoor?" Marcus asked.

"I'm not sure." Pablo hung the lantern back up where he had found it, and turned the dial until the light diminished. "Let's get out of here and then we can figure it out." Pablo climbed out first, and Marcus trailed behind him. Once they were at the top, they dusted themselves off.

Pablo wandered around the barn looking for something to attach to the trapdoor so that they could lift the dropped end up out of the hole. Marcus went to the other side of the barn and kicked some hay into a small pile. He then turned to see if Pablo was looking. Once it was safe, he dropped the bottle into the hay and quickly covered it up. He went back to where Pablo was. "Find anything?"

"Well, here's some rope. We can tie it around the door and lift it that way."

"Okay, let's give it a shot," said Marcus.

Pablo went down into the hole and Marcus dropped the rope down. Pablo fumbled his way around the edge of the door with the rope. He managed to slide it underneath and then he pulled up the two ends and tied a knot in the center. Then he tossed the ends up to Marcus.

"Okay, I'm coming up." Once Pablo was out of the hole, the boys each pulled an end of the rope. The door slowly rose upwards. It creaked and groaned; it sounded like the other end was going to collapse next.

"I see the end of it!" Marcus almost let go of the rope. It was heavier than he had expected.

"Marcus, steady yourself!"

The boys continued to raise the door until it was almost to the top of the opening.

"This isn't going to work!" Pablo said suddenly. "We need something to keep it in place!"

They quickly looked around the barn. They would have to tie the rope to the wall and look for a long piece of wood to place under the front end, so that it wouldn't fall into the hole.

"Marcus, you hold onto the rope the best you can. I'm going to run out and get a slat off the fence to brace the door with."

Marcus nodded. "Don't take too long. I don't know how long I can hold this!"

Pablo let go of his end slowly while Marcus gripped it harder.

"I'll be right back!" Pablo ran to the front of the barn and removed the piece of wood holding the door closed. He would have used it but it wasn't long enough. He opened the door slowly, hoping his mother wouldn't see him. He looked from left to right and then right to left. Once he knew it was clear, he ran out to the back of the barn. He carefully climbed over the thistle bush. Although it didn't matter how careful he was, he knew he would end up with thistles in places that were most uncomfortable. He squirmed as the thistles poked him. He reached up to one of the slats on the fence and pulled as hard, and as fast as he could, until the wood loosened. He fell backwards—right into the thistle bush. "Ouch, ouch, ouch, shit!" Pablo got up as quickly as he could, and ran frantically back inside the barn. Marcus was standing there sweating and swearing.

"Close the door, Pablo!" Marcus yelled. "Quick, get over here. The rope is slipping!"

Pablo closed the door behind him. His hands were burning from the thistles. He ran over to where Marcus was. "Okay, when I say pull, you need to use all your strength, and I'll place the board underneath it, okay?"

"Okay, hurry up!" Marcus pleaded.

Pablo went over to the open end of the hole and situated himself so that he could slide the board underneath the edge of the trapdoor while Marcus lifted it.

"Okay ... one, two, three, pull!" Pablo yelled.

Marcus took in a deep breath, grunted, and pulled with all his strength. The door lifted slowly and got stuck at the opening because the rope was too thick.

"Come on, Marcus pull!" Pablo shouted. Marcus continued grunting and groaning and then pulled again as hard as he could. Finally, the door squeezed its way up through the hole and Pablo slid the slat underneath.

"Got it!" Pablo said. "Good work, Marcus!"

Marcus fell backwards onto his ass! He was out of breath. His muscles were weak. Pablo got up and went over to see if he was okay.

Marcus got up on his feet while Pablo removed the rope that was tied around the trapdoor. He tossed it into the corner of a stall. "Okay Marcus, let's get out of here."

The boys moved the crate back on top of the trapdoor. Pablo picked up the book and stuffed it under his shirt. They rushed out of the barn and closed the door. They were both sweating and out of breath. Thankfully, there was no one on the back porch. The boys laughed quietly, and they slowed their pace as they walked towards the house.

When they were about thirty feet away from the barn, they heard a loud *Crash!* behind them. Pablo and Marcus ran back and burst into the barn. They ran over to where the crate *had* been sitting; it was down in the hole! The crate and the trapdoor had collapsed from the weight.

"Oh shit, Pablo! What are we going to do now!?" He sat down and was almost in tears. "We're screwed!"

Pablo thought for a bit. "Hey Marcus, maybe it's a good thing that the crate fell through. This way, they won't know we had pried our way in." Marcus was amazed sometimes with his brother's ideas.

"I guess you could be right," Marcus said. "Okay, let's just leave it the way it is and get the hell out of here!"

Pablo agreed.

The boys ran back out of the barn and shut the door. When they reached the house they rushed up to the loft.

"Man, that was close!" Marcus plopped himself down on his bed.

Pablo pulled the book out from under his shirt. He sat on the edge of his bed and opened it. The writing and pictures were clearer now that he was in better light. It had the smell of dust and old paper. He would have to be careful turning the pages, because they seemed extremely brittle. Marcus sat beside Pablo. They flipped through the pages of the book looking at some of the photos.

"Hold it, turn back a page," Marcus said.

Pablo turned the page and looked at the picture that Marcus had pointed out. "It almost looks like San Rafael, doesn't it?" Pablo said. Marcus nodded. "It sure does. Maybe we can make out who some of the bikers are?"

The boys stared at the photo for a while, until Pablo thought he saw his dad in the photo. "No, it can't be, can it?"

"Can't be what, Pablo?"

"Dad?" Pablo said.

Marcus looked at where Pablo pointed. "Maybe."

"Yeah, it is a bit fuzzy and hard to tell. It sure would answer a lot of questions if it was him," Pablo said.

Rosalia had heard the boys come in, so she headed up to the loft. She knocked lightly on their door. She respected their privacy. Pablo quickly shoved the book under his mattress and then called for her to come in.

"Yah?" Pablo said.

"Hey, boys." Rosalia walked in.

"Everything okay, Momma?" asked Pablo as he stood up.

"I received a call from the hospital where your uncle is. They want you to pick up him up in the morning, Pablo. Would that be okay?"

"Yes, sure," said Pablo, with excitement in his voice.

"Can I go too?" Marcus asked.

"No, not this time, son. There won't be enough room. Next time Pablo goes to town you can go with him." Rosalia was going to say yes, but then she realized it would be a snug fit for the three of them in the front of the truck. George would need space to stretch out.

Marcus was disappointed, but he said, "Okay, Momma." He enjoyed going away from the farm. It was as if it was just the two of them leaving and going their own way. It was a free feeling.

"Don't stay up too late," she said, as she shut the door behind her.

Bernice returned to George's room with a tray of food. He wasn't hoping for anything great, because of the hospital crap he had earlier that day. She removed the lid and placed the tray in front of him.

"Luckily, we had a warmer that worked tonight," she said. "I hope it's okay."

George looked at the food. It looked reasonable, until he started eating it. He didn't want to spit it out with Bernice in the room, so he took his time and pretended to chew what was in his mouth. It was hot, but the food had a rubber texture to it. He managed to get a few bites down this time, but only because of what Bernice had said earlier. He wanted to get out of there. With that thought, he pushed the tray away and just said that his stomach wasn't feeling well. He would be thankful to taste Rosalia's cooking again. Just the thought of it made his mouth water. The nurse took the tray away and placed it on the counter. "Bernardo won't be coming to get you in the morning. His wife said he was away."

"Oh? Gone again is he?" George responded.

"Does he go away often?"

"Yes, he works out of town for long periods at a time."

"His wife said that Pablo would come and pick you up."

"Great! He's an awesome boy—damn near a man. He has grown so much in the last year."

That evening, Andrea was back on shift. She had gotten George up on his feet. She needed him to start moving around tonight, so that she would be confident in letting him leave in the morning. "Put your weight on me," she said.

"I'm trying, but you're so ... short." He laughed. "I'm going to fall on top of you." George was a very tall man and towered over most people.

"Don't worry about it. I'm used to this," she said, as she supported him.

George had a hard time putting his weight on her. He didn't feel right doing it. He ended up putting most of it on his bad side and almost fell over. She caught him, and then she looked at him sternly. "Put your weight on me!" She put his arm back around her shoulders and pulled him towards her. He hadn't been this close to a woman in a long time. He had many thoughts going through his head, and most of the time he had a hard time keeping them to himself.

"It wouldn't be a bad thing if I fell on top of you."

Andrea tried to ignore his comment and encouraged him to stay focused on walking. They hobbled around the room a couple of times before he had had enough. Andrea positioned him so that he could sit back on the bed. He sat down carefully while she held him. Once down, she let go and backed off. "So, how was that?"

"Well ...," He took a breath. "It was okay, although a bit harder than I'd expected."

The doctor will want to see you in about ten days, so he can see how your side is healing," she said. "We'll make sure you have enough pain medication so that you won't have to run out to get any until you see the doctor."

"Okay," George answered. "Thank you!"

It was starting to get dark outside and the nurse suggested to George that he should try to get a good night's sleep. Tomorrow would be a long day for him. She left the room and returned with his medication for the night. Once he was positioned and comfortable, she turned out the light and told him she would be back in a couple of hours to check on him. George closed his eyes. *It's going to be good to be out of this room and back on the farm*, he thought.

chapter

11

"OKAY, MOMMA. I'm heading out to pick up Uncle George." Pablo walked past her on the front porch.

She gave him a pat on the shoulder. "See you soon, son."

Pablo backed the truck out of the yard and headed down the road to the hospital.

Marcus was sitting beside his Momma on the front porch. "Is Uncle George okay?"

Rosalia turned to Marcus with concern in her eyes. "I hope so, Marcus."

"What happened?" he asked, hoping she would tell him.

"I'm not sure, son. Your dad didn't say anything. I'm sure your Uncle George will tell us." She patted him on the leg and got up from the chair. "I need to go make sure his room is ready for when he gets here."

Marcus watched her go into the farmhouse, and then he looked towards the road as the trail of dust settled in the distance. The truck disappeared around the corner towards town.

Boss and Spud arrived at the hospital around 9:30 A.M. Boss walked up to the admissions desk and asked the woman where he would find George Gomez. The nurse looked up George's file. "It looks like Mr. Gomez is being discharged this morning. You may wait over there in the waiting area." The nurse pointed to her right.

Boss glanced over to where she pointed and then nodded. He didn't want to make a commotion and alarm anyone as to why they were there. He walked over to the waiting area and motioned for Spud to join him. They sat down on some chairs that were facing the desk. This way they would see when George was coming out.

"So, he is being released today, Spud," Boss said, as he nudged him.

"Wow, talk about being here at the right time," Spud answered. "Do you think someone else is picking him up?"

"Yes, most likely," Boss said. "They won't let him leave on his own—I don't think."

Pablo tuned the radio station to the local one. *They are so boring*, he thought. He switched it off. It was more irritating than enjoyable. Ten minutes later, he rounded the next corner towards the hospital. There weren't many vehicles out front, so it was easy to find a parking spot. He was thankful for this, because he still wasn't comfortable driving the truck into small spots. He pulled in and parked.

The front door to the hospital opened and a teenager, about the age of sixteen, walked in. He looked as if he was lost. Pablo had never been to this hospital before.

Boss and Spud watched the teen intently. Pablo saw them looking at him, and he quickly turned his head. He had noticed the men were wearing leather vests. *Must be bikers, just like in the book we found. Why are they here?* he wondered.

The men kept staring at Pablo. Pablo was getting nervous and his stomach started flipping. The bikers noticed his apprehension. They liked making people nervous; it made them feel powerful.

Pablo walked in the opposite direction of the bikers until he spotted the front desk. He quickened his pace.

The bikers decided to give him a rest and focused back on the entranceway of the hospital—waiting patiently for a familiar face, so that they would know who was picking up George.

Pablo stood at the front desk until someone showed up. He stared ahead and didn't dare look back.

"Yes son, how may I help you?" a woman said, startling him.

Pablo looked at her. He was lost for words. He gulped and took in a deep breath. "I'm here to pick up my uncle." It took a lot to make Pablo nervous, and he couldn't figure out why these bikers made him feel this way.

"Your uncle's name is?" She pulled a chart off the wall.

"His name is George. George Gomez," said Pablo.

Boss nudged Spud to get his attention. "It's him," he said.

Spud looked over at Boss, "Who?"

"George's nephew. He must be here to pick him up."

The nurse thumbed through the names on the chart. "Your uncle will be out shortly. You may have a seat in the waiting area."

"Thank you, Miss," Pablo said. *Thank god I don't have to wait long*, he thought. He stood there for a moment and then got his courage up. He walked over to where Boss and Spud were sitting, and he sat down in the farthest seat, facing the front door. He wished he could have sat facing the desk, but there were no chairs available. He felt nauseous. He could sense their penetrating stares. Pablo was concentrating so hard on avoiding the bikers that he didn't notice his uncle being wheeled into the waiting area. There was a slight commotion where the bikers were sitting, but Pablo didn't dare look. From the little he had read about bikers, he already knew not to interfere with them—no matter what they were doing.

Boss and Spud had quickly risen to their feet when they spotted George being wheeled in. They walked up to him. George was a bit confused, because he was expecting his nephew to pick him up. He looked around but couldn't see past Boss and Spud. Spud looked at George, and when no one was looking, he motioned to George to zip his lip and not say a word. George knew better than to argue with these two men.

Pablo couldn't help it, he finally turned his head. He had to see what was going on. When he looked, he spotted the bikers standing with their backs towards him. He didn't notice that they were standing in front of George.

The nurse who had pushed George out in the wheelchair held out his chart. She read it over quickly. She read that George's nephew was to pick him up. "Are you George's nephew?" She knew this was a dumb question seeing that Boss and Spud were about the same age, or even older than George.

Boss kept his voice low. "No miss, his nephew couldn't make it. He called us to come and pick him up. I believe he had truck problems."

Pablo tried to hear what they were saying, but he was too far away.

The nurse glanced over at the front desk. The nurse who was there must have gone on her break. The nurse was hesitant to let George go with these men, but felt they were telling her the truth, even though they were intimidating. She passed the chart to Boss to sign. "It's regulations. We require a signature when discharging a patient." She figured if anything came of it, at least she had his signature and would be able to track him down.

Boss took the chart and pen and quickly scribbled a signature. The nurse gave Boss instructions as to the further care George needed. She said good-bye to George and gave the men the okay that he was ready to leave. She returned down the hall with the chart.

Boss got behind the wheelchair and started pushing it. As they passed Pablo, Spud walked along the right side of the wheelchair so George couldn't see Pablo; however, Pablo saw George. Pablo froze! He didn't know what to do or say. As the bikers passed Pablo, they just glared at him, as if to say, "Fuck off, and don't even try it!" Pablo looked quickly away from them until they were out the door. He watched as they loaded George into an SUV. When they finally left the parking lot, Pablo went back to the front desk. He waited a bit until the nurse who had been attending George came out.

"Who were those men?" Pablo asked.

"Oh, they were friends of a patient." She went to go back to what she was doing. She looked back up at Pablo. He displayed a very confused look.

"And you are ...?" she asked.

"Pablo. Pablo Gomez. I was supposed to pick up my uncle. His name is George Gomez. He just left with those two bikers." Pablo had no idea what he was going to do. These bikers worried him. "Do you know where they took my uncle?"

The nurse swallowed hard. She looked down at George's chart again, and it had specifically said that George's nephew was picking him up. She felt like shit.

"I'm sorry son, they didn't say where they were going. I assume they're taking him home?" She was now just as confused as Pablo was.

"I hope he'll be okay," Pablo added.

"I'm sure he will. She had to stay positive and believe that she did the right thing. She got up off the chair and stood beside Pablo. She put her arm around his shoulder as she walked him out of the hospital. "It'll be okay," she said, trying to reassure him.

Pablo nodded and waved good-bye to the nurse as she closed the door. He looked down the road. The SUV was no where in sight.

Boss pulled the SUV into the back parking lot of the clubhouse. There were a few bikes parked near the back door.

"Whiskey, how are you doing?" Boss asked.

George nodded his head, as if to say 'fine.'

"Spud, may I have a word with you?" Boss said.

"Sure, Boss. We'll be just a minute, Whiskey." Boss and Spud got out of the SUV and went into the building. Boss looked out to make sure there was no one else following. He closed the door behind him.

George was a bit concerned as to what was going on. He wondered if he should take off now that he had the chance.

"Okay," Boss said, "we need to get Whiskey in here. I'm not sure how he will feel about it. He doesn't look well."

"Look Boss, is there anything else we can do besides interrogate him?" Spud asked.

"Unfortunately, no. We can't take any chances and you know that. We'll take him to the room down the hall. Now, go get him."

Spud nodded.

Boss slapped him on the back. "That-a-boy!"

Spud walked out of the building and back to the SUV. "You may as well come in for a bit. No sense you sitting out here in the heat."

George looked at Spud. "No, that's okay. I'll just wait here."

Spud opened the door to the SUV and held out his hand to help George out. "Hey man, I know you're hurting, but I'm not sure how long we are going to be here. You may as well come in for a few."

George wasn't sure what was up, and it was getting a little warm sitting there. He decided to follow Spud into the building. He hadn't been in the clubhouse since he had met with the other bikers a week or so ago; he couldn't remember. The place gave him the creeps. It never used to, but after what he'd been through, he didn't feel like he trusted any of them. Spud led him into the back room where Boss had gone.

Once inside the room the door was shut behind them. George noticed three other bikers across the room. They had looked up when they entered. They were full-patched members. Boss walked over to them and asked them to wait outside. There was no need for them to listen to what was going on. Spud locked the door after they left. George looked back as he heard the click.

"Have a seat, Whiskey," Boss instructed.

George sat down in the chair across from Boss.

"I know you know what this is all about," Boss started to say. George looked at him blankly.

"What we need to know, Whiskey, is what happened to you? Who sent you out?" Boss asked.

George tried to think. He couldn't remember. He had a feeling this wasn't what they were looking for. He wasn't able to tell them anything. George moved in his chair a bit; he was uncomfortable and his side was throbbing. He hadn't had any medication since early that morning and it was starting to show.

"We have reason to believe that you have discussed things about the *family* with others," Boss interrogated. "Is this correct?"

George stared at him. "Boss, I have no idea what you're talking about."

"What do you mean you don't know?" Boss was getting annoyed.

"I don't know! Honest, I can't remember."

"Can't remember?" Boss huffed around the room. "He can't remember, Spud. Did you hear that? We've heard this before, and I'm sorry to say, this is not a good cover-up. Anyone can say 'I can't remember,' just so they don't have to admit to anything." There was a moment of silence. "Well, I'm telling you, I'm not going to buy it!" Boss couldn't handle it when people said things like this. He's been there before. Even if it was true, he still couldn't take the chance. "Okay, fine. If that's the way you want to play it, then we have no choice but to let you go."

"Let me go?" George was confused.

"Yes, let you go. Spud, pass me that paper, will ya?"

Spud went into one of the filing cabinets and pulled out a folder. In the folder was a piece of paper. Spud passed it to Boss. Boss unfolded it and then passed it to George. "Read it." Boss sat back down on the chair while George read what was written on the paper.

A few minutes later, George looked up. Boss tossed a pen at him. "Sign it!"

George showed hesitation but then signed it. In a way he was relieved that he would no longer be a part of 'Riders of Reason.' He could now have a life.

"Did you read it all?"

George nodded, and he gave the paper and pen to Boss. Boss rose and passed them to Spud. "You're free to go. Oh and another thing ..." Boss got up and pulled out a leather vest from the closet. He dropped it on the table in front of George. George looked at it. It was his vest.

"Where did you find this?" George asked.

Boss glared at him. "You're shitting me, right? I mean, you really don't remember?"

"No, Boss," George said.

George turned the vest over and noticed the chapter patches were missing.

"Well, we can't take any chances, George. We still have to let you go."

George had wished to be free of the club, but suddenly he felt a great loss. He had thought of these men as brothers, now he couldn't even talk to them. Boss went to the side door and opened it.

"We're done," he said to the others outside.

The bikers outside glanced up and then went back inside. The atmosphere was stale. Boss and Spud escorted George back to the SUV.

chapter

12

PABLO SEARCHED for about an hour and had no luck in finding his uncle. He noticed bikers off and on, but they appeared to be just riding through town and not stopping. His mother would be worried by now, so he figured he better head back home. He turned the truck around and headed down the dirt road. As he drove, he daydreamed about his dad and if he would ever be home permanently. Deep down he knew it was a lost dream.

Pablo reached the farmhouse around noon. He guessed he had most likely missed lunch. He parked the truck and quickly scanned the driveway. There was no sign of any other vehicle coming in or leaving. Pablo walked into the house to find his mother standing in front of him.

"Pablo! I was worried about you!" She hugged him tightly. "What took you so long?"

"Momma, I'm fine." Pablo pushed his way inside. She was domineering at times.

"I'm sorry," she said. "Where's George?"

"Momma, I have no idea. I searched all over for him, but I don't know where they took him."

"What do you mean? Where *who* took him? Son, what are you talking about?"

Pablo sat on the sofa. "Momma, I went to pick him up, but two other men were there and Uncle George left with them."

"Two other men? Who were they?"

Pablo didn't want to tell her that the men were bikers. "No idea, Momma."

"Okay Pablo, don't worry. I'm sure George will show up soon. Lunch is almost ready, but it's a bit late today."

"No problem. Where's Marcus?" Pablo asked, as he headed into the kitchen behind her.

"He's up in the loft. You can holler at him to come down."

Pablo went up to the loft instead of hollering. He walked into their room and found Marcus reading a magazine. "Hey, Marcus."

Marcus looked up. "Hey."

"Lunch is ready."

"Not hungry."

"What do you mean you're not hungry? Aren't you feeling well?"

"Yeah, I'm fine. Go on without me."

"Okay, but Momma will want to know why." Pablo went back downstairs and into the kitchen. His mother had already set the table for three. "Marcus won't be coming down."

"Oh? Why?"

"Not sure, he said he wasn't hungry."

Rosalia was concerned. *Nothing* seemed to be going right today. It didn't surprise her.

"Okay." She put down some cheese sandwiches and a pot of chicken soup. "Help yourself, son." She sat down across from him.

Marcus tossed the magazine onto the floor and lay back on his bed. He didn't understand what was going on, and why his stepmother would never tell him anything, when she would always discuss things with Pablo. This hurt Marcus quite a bit. He felt like a loner a lot of the time. Pablo was favoured. He couldn't wait until he was old enough to leave the farm for good. Even though he was only fourteen, he felt like he could handle himself in the outside world.

Just as Pablo finished the last bite of his sandwich, he heard a vehicle pull in. "Momma! I think Uncle George is home!"

They jumped up from the table and ran out to the front door. They saw two men wearing leather vests helping George out of the SUV. Rosalia stood inside. She didn't like the looks of the men. Pablo headed for the door.

"Son, please be careful," Rosalia said.

"I will, Momma," Pablo said. He opened the screen door, ran down the steps and out to the end of the driveway to help his uncle. He glared at the two men. He had found a bit of courage standing alongside his uncle. Marcus heard the commotion downstairs and glanced out of his window. He was happy to see that his uncle was home. He had forgotten that he had been pouting and ran down to greet him. George hobbled while Pablo helped him struggle up the steps. Marcus held the door open for them. Boss and Spud got back into the truck and quickly drove off. They didn't want any confrontation. Boss didn't feel good about letting George go, but he couldn't take the chance of him getting hurt or even killed. Boss had to hide his personal emotions from all the members. He wished he'd known what had happened. It wasn't the end, and he was determined to find out who was responsible.

Rosalia was watching them leave from the porch. Once George was inside, Pablo steadied him until he could sit down.

"You're back!" Rosalia said. When George was comfortable, she gave him a hug.

"Yes," he said, as he gasped for a breath.

"How are you, George?" Rosalia sat beside him and held his hand. "We've been so worried about you." You could see the gleam in Rosalia's eyes. They sparkled with excitement.

Marcus sat down on the far side of the sofa as he watched quietly.

George pointed to a small round stool in the corner beside the woodstove. It had a good layer of foam on it, covered by some old, tattered textile-type fabric.

"Marcus, would you please bring that stool over here, so that I can rest my legs on it?" Marcus got up and pulled the stool closer to his uncle. He sat down on the floor beside him.

"Is this okay?" Marcus looked approvingly up at him.

"Yes, thank you, Marcus."

"So, you don't have to leave anymore?" Pablo asked.

"No, I'm here for a while," George answered.

"What happened? I mean, were you in an accident?" Marcus asked.

"I can't answer that question," he said. "I wish I could."

Pablo sat back on the sofa. He wanted to ask so many questions, especially about the bikers, but he knew it wasn't the right time.

George spent the rest of the day relaxing, while the boys went outside to finish their chores. They were told to stay out of George's hair. He would be able to spend more time with Rosalia and the boys now that he was free of the motorcycle club.

Since George wasn't able to sleep that night, he decided to get up. He stumbled out of his room, and found Rosalia fast asleep on the sofa. She looked so worn-out. He felt sorry for her and the boys. As he hobbled on the wooden floors, they creaked, which startled Rosalia. She opened her eyes and tried to focus. She saw George standing there. "George, are you okay?"

"Yes, Rosa."

"Here, let me help you." She quickly rose to her feet.

George nodded. "No, I can do it."

Rosalia sat back down on the sofa and rubbed her eyes. "I must have fallen asleep. What time is it?"

"It's 3:00." He sat down beside her. They sat quietly for a bit. "So, when's Bernardo coming home?" he asked.

Rosalia shrugged her shoulders. George could sense the tension when he mentioned Bernardo's name. "Are you sure you're okay, Rosa?" She leaned forward and cupped her face in her hands. She wasn't okay and George knew it. He placed his arm around her shoulder and pulled her closer to him. "I know, Hon. It's gotta be so hard having him away all the time."

Rosalia leaned into George and started sobbing. George held her for a few minutes until she was ready to talk. She sat back and held his hand tightly. "George, I have to tell you something."

"Sure, anything." He caressed her hand. It had been years since his last long-term relationship, and Rosalia was the only woman that he was able to let close to him. Holding her hand in his made him feel good all over. She was a very pretty woman and deserved so much better in life. His brother, Bernardo, was a good husband at bringing in the money, but he wasn't good at keeping the bond between them alive. George listened intently as to what Rosalia had to say. She wiped her eyes with her other hand, because she didn't want to let go of George's hand. She squeezed tighter. "George, this is silly." She suddenly felt guilty about what she was about to tell him. "I was so worried about you."

George held her closer. The lavender scent she was wearing drew him in even more. "Yes, I know you were, Rosa. I'm sorry I put you through all this."

"What happened?" Rosalia asked.

"Hon, I'm not sure. But when I find out, you'll be the first to know."

"Well, I'm so happy you're home and alive."

"It's good to be home. And hey, those boys are growing like crazy." He tried to cheer her up a bit.

Rosalia smiled. "Yes, they sure are. They have been so good the last few months at handling everything around here while you and Bernardo have been away."

"They're turning into fine young men," George added.

"If it hadn't been for you, George, they probably would have left home a long time ago. You have given them the respect and companionship that they need."

George felt sudden warmth fill him. He knew the boys loved him, but he had never realized he had that kind of effect on them. "That's great, Rosa. I will be here for quite a while now. I won't be leaving. I am dedicating my time to you, the boys, and the farm."

Rosalia smiled. She never expected this from George. "George, I just realized you didn't have your motorcycle when you came in. *Were* you in an accident?"

George was quiet for a moment. He never even thought about his bike, until now. "Oh, yeah ... Rosa, I completely forgot about my bike. To be honest, I don't think I was in an accident. As for the bike, I haven't a clue. Once I start getting around more, I will have to see what I can find out. But for now, I'm not going anywhere."

Rosalia felt calm around George. She knew in her heart that things would be okay.

"You should get some sleep, Hon." George rubbed her shoulders.

"Yes, I know." She decided what she really wanted to tell him would have to wait until a later time. "I think I can sleep now."

George smiled and helped her up off the sofa. He let her lean on him as he led her to her bedroom. George went over and pulled the sheet down for her. Once she was in bed, he put the sheet up over her and kissed her on the cheek. "Good night, Rosa."

She closed her eyes. Sleep would come.

George went back into his room and closed the door. It wouldn't be long and the boys would be up.

It had been a few days since George had returned home. He was starting to feel much better and could move around more without any help. He sat on the back porch watching the evening sun go down. Even though the harvest was finished, there were still chores to do around the farm. The boys were taking advantage of their time off and were already upstairs in their room. Rosalia was busy cleaning the kitchen after dinner.

Marcus sat on the edge of his bed. "Hey Pablo, we outta pick ourselves out a couple of motorcycles. Whadda ya think?"

Pablo was sitting in a nearby chair reading the first few pages of 'Riders of Reason.' The boys had dreams of owning their own motorcycle just like their uncle. It was in their blood and they desired it. Pablo tossed the book onto the table, and went and sat on his bed. "Yeah ... I think it's about time, too. How do you think we can swing it?"

"Well, we do have quite a bit of money saved from working. I'm sure Momma would let us spend some of it."

"I don't know about that," Pablo said. "But we could ask her."

"I read in the newspaper that they hold swap meets about a mile from here, on Sundays," Marcus said. "Maybe we could go out there this weekend?"

Pablo lay back on the bed and put his arms behind his head. He hadn't bothered his mother yet about buying a bike and wasn't sure how to go about it. He didn't want to upset her. He thought about it for a bit. "I guess it can't hurt to ask." Pablo sat back up and then tossed a pillow across the room hitting Marcus in the head.

"Hey!" Marcus shouted, and he threw it back at him.

"Watch it!" Pablo laughed. He liked to bug Marcus from time to time, because he was so easy to pester. Marcus jumped up, flew across the bed and wrestled Pablo until they both fell to the floor. They struggled for some time until there was a loud knock on the door. Their momma walked in. "What's going on in here!" She couldn't help but laugh. She would love to have joined them, but someone had to be the adult. "Time to calm down and get some sleep."

"Sure, Momma." They jumped up and went back to their own beds.

"Hey, Momma, do you think we could spend some of our savings?" Pablo decided that asking directly for a motorcycle wouldn't work.

"Well, you boys are getting old enough to make your own decisions, you know that right?"

The boys looked at each other and then back at their momma. "Yes ... m'am," said Pablo. Marcus nodded in agreement.

"Well, I figure you both have worked so hard on the farm that I'll let you buy whatever you want from your savings, how about that?"

The boys almost went hysterical and had a hard time holding the excitement in.

"That's great, Momma! Thank you!" They couldn't believe what they just heard.

"Now, it's time to get some sleep," she said.

"Night, Momma!" they both said.

Once she left the room, the boys were so excited that there was no way they would get any sleep that night. They tossed and turned, until finally, they both grabbed some magazines and were dreaming about the bike they wanted. They finally dozed off around 2 A.M. In the morning, the boys rushed down to the kitchen to grab a bite to eat. Their uncle and mother weren't awake yet, but it was a bit early. Pablo put some coffee on and Marcus grabbed some biscuits out of the breadbox. They loved toasted biscuits with butter in the morning. They sat down across from each other at the table, eating their breakfast and sipping their coffee. Fifteen minutes later, their uncle strolled into the kitchen. "You boys sleep well?"

"Not really," Pablo said. "It was kind of hard to sleep last night."

"Oh? And why is that?" George picked up a mug and filled it with coffee. He went over and sat down with the boys.

"What was it like when you bought your first bike, Uncle George?" Marcus asked curiously.

Their uncle looked out of the kitchen window as though he was dreaming. He started twirling the end of his goatee with his fingers.

"Well ... it was the most thrilling thing that happened to me as a teenager. I remember not sleeping for days, knowing that my time was coming to buy my very first bike. Why do you ask?"

Pablo spoke up before Marcus could say anything. "Momma said that we could spend our savings on anything we wanted."

"Oh, did she now? Did she say you could buy bikes?"

"Well, not exactly," Pablo started, "but she did say we could buy anything." Pablo was hoping that his uncle wasn't going to say something to their momma to stop them from buying them.

George sipped his coffee. He knew the boys were responsible, but at the same time, he knew how Rosalia and Bernardo felt about motorcycles. The boys were old enough to make their choices, but George wanted this to be a safe decision. And, after his near-death experience, he felt protective.

"Okay, Pablo, since your momma didn't say you couldn't buy bikes, I'm going to take you boys shopping. Is that okay?" George said.

The boys looked at each other. "Really? You would do that for us?" Pablo said excitedly. Marcus was revealing a huge shit-eating grin; he was ecstatic.

"Yes, I would love too!" George said. "I know what you boys

are going through, and I am so glad I'll be there to see you purchase your first ones! I think it is very important, and a big decision. There is nothing better than riding in the wind on your very own ride."

The boys felt how proud their uncle was because he owned and rode a hawg. It was as if nothing in the world could beat it. They felt they were making a very good decision, especially with their uncle behind them one-hundred percent.

"We'll head out around ten," he told the boys. "Now listen," he said in a hushed voice, "we need to keep this quiet. I'll explain it to your momma when we get home." As he got up from the table he rubbed the top of Pablo's head. "You both are growing into decent young men, and I'm proud of you." He placed his empty mug on the counter and went into the sitting room.

Marcus and Pablo quickly got up from the table. It would be a few hours before they headed off, and they needed to occupy themselves with something. They put their dishes in the sink and raced each other back up to the loft.

chapter

13

ROSALIA WAS BUSY IN THE KITCHEN combining ingredients in a bowl so that they could have fresh bread with their dinner that night. The boys kissed her on their way out the door. George was already in the truck waiting for them. He had told her that he was taking the boys to town, but he didn't say what they were shopping for.

"Get in boys," George said. "Let's go to town!" Usually the boys would only go to town for supplies, so this was quite a treat for them. They waved to their Momma who was now standing on the front porch. She smiled at the three of them as they drove off. All George had said to Rosalia was that he was taking the boys shopping.

When they arrived in town, the streets were just starting to wake up. The local café had a few people sitting outside having their morning coffee. It was a very small but historical town.

"It sure looks different when you're not driving," Pablo said, as he glanced around at the stores.

"Now, look at that lass!" Their uncle pointed to a girl around the age of twenty, wearing a pair of tattered jean shorts and a skimpy pink halter top and sandals. Her long blonde hair bounced off the top of her shoulders as she nonchalantly pranced along the sidewalk. She gazed around as if she owned the place, knowing that she made heads turn as her hips swayed back and forth in opposite rhythm of her chest.

The boys looked at where he was pointing. She was a looker all right. The boys smiled and stared just as long as their uncle did. She winked at them as the truck passed her.

"Take after your uncle after all." George rubbed the top of Marcus' head and chuckled.

The motorcycle store was about ten minutes away on the outskirts of town. The boys had never been there. There were bikes parked out front and inside the store. Pablo didn't expect the building to be as big as it was.

George pulled into the parking lot. The boys jumped out of the truck as fast as they could. They couldn't believe their eyes. The bikes were beautiful and so shiny. George guided the boys away from the newer bikes, because they were too expensive for their first ones.

"Okay boys, we'll have to go over to the used ones," George said. "As you can see, the prices of the new bikes are very high."

The boys agreed and followed their uncle. They walked around to the back of the building to where they stored the used bikes. There was a mechanic outside working on one of them. George walked up to him and told him what he was looking for. The mechanic led them over to a couple of bikes. They weren't as polished as the other ones they'd seen. They were slightly rusted and had a few dents in the tanks. Marcus was a bit disappointed after looking at the new ones, but he had to bite his tongue. "We can fix 'em up, right Pablo?" he whispered.

Pablo nodded.

Their uncle was in discussion with a salesman who appeared from around the corner. He walked over to the boys after a bit. The salesman stayed where he was.

"Well boys, we can take a look at these two. He pointed to a couple of Honda 250's. They're both good starter bikes."

Marcus and Pablo went over to the Honda's and looked them over.

"Have a seat on them!" the salesman hollered from across the lot.

Marcus looked at his uncle approvingly. "Can we?"

"Yes, of course." George instructed the boys how to sit on the bikes and hold them steady without dropping them.

"Well, how do they fit?" the salesperson asked, as he walked over to them.

The boys had ear-to-ear grins. They had nothing to say, except yes. They wanted them. There was no hesitation. George instructed the boys to get off again. He wanted to fire the bikes up and have a look at them more closely before he made the final decision. Marcus and Pablo went and sat down on a nearby bench. Their legs were jumping up and down. Their excitement was unbelievable.

After George thoroughly looked over the bikes and was satisfied they would be okay for the boys, he went into the store with the salesman to finish the deal. He came back out about twenty minutes later with two sets of keys.

"How much were they, George?" Pablo asked.

Their uncle smiled and said, "Don't worry, you boys had enough."

Pablo knew that meant not to say another word. The salesman came out and helped their uncle load the bikes into the back of the truck. It would be a slow ride home, but the boys didn't care. They couldn't help but look back in the truck bed off and on to see the bikes. It was like a dream come true.

They arrived home just before lunch. As they pulled into the driveway, their mother came out the front door, tea towel in hand. George parked the truck and turned it off. The three of them jumped out.

Rosalia noticed the back of the truck. She went running out to see. She swallowed hard. "Oh my Lord, George! How ... how could you?"

"Rosa dear, the boys are old enough to make their own choices. I didn't tell them to buy the bikes, it was what they wanted. I figured if this is what they truly wanted, then I would go with them and help them out."

"But, but ... George." She was lost for words. Tears filled her eyes. The only thing she could see was her sons dying on the road somewhere. She never approved of motorcycles and hated that George even rode one. She ran inside the house, and the door slammed behind her. The boys felt terrible. What had they done? They looked regretfully at their uncle.

George put his arm around Marcus and squeezed his shoulders. "Don't worry, it'll be okay. Give me a moment with your momma." He went into the house behind her.

Marcus and Pablo sat on the tailgate of the truck and stared out onto the road.

"Do you think it was a good idea, Pablo?" Marcus asked.

Pablo was quiet. He too didn't feel good about what they did. They should have told their mother what they were doing. At least then, she would have known and would have been able to deal with it better.

"Rosa?" George put his arms around her and held her close. She wanted to push him away, but she needed him. She sobbed in his arms.

"I'm so scared, George. I don't want the boys hurt. I don't want them taking off like you did for days on end without telling me where they're going."

George tried to reassure her that it wasn't going to happen, and that what he did was very different from what the boys would use the bikes for. *How am I going to explain this?* he thought. "Look Rosa, the boys will need a license to ride on the roads. How about I promise you that they won't get their license for at least six months? They'll still be able to ride around the farm. That way, it'll give them some experience before they do get their license, and you can keep your eye on them while they're learning. You or Bernardo will have to sign for their license. How does that sound?"

Rosalia thought about what George just said. She still didn't approve, but then the boys would do what they wanted soon anyways. At least they wouldn't be on the roads for at least six months to a year. She trusted George. "Okay, George. Please promise me they won't be out there for at least six months."

"I promise you. Thank you, Rosa. You know, I wish you had been with us today when the boys sat on those bikes. They were the happiest boys I have seen in a long time. I've never seen them so excited. They were proud of buying them and they have worked so hard."

Rosalia smiled. She agreed that they did earn them; she had to work through her own fears now. George leaned over to give her a kiss on the cheek, but instead, he turned her face towards his and he kissed her on the lips. It seemed so natural.

Rosalia stood quietly. *George kissed her in a way he had never kissed her before.* She smiled sweetly at him.

George looked into her eyes, and she could sense that he had strong feelings for her. She, too, was starting to feel more for him. She couldn't help but feel guilty. He headed out the door to see the boys. Rosalia held back some deep emotions and wiped her eyes.

Marcus and Pablo heard the front door close. They looked back and their uncle headed down the steps towards them.

"Well?" Pablo said hesitantly.

"It's all good, boys. I had to promise your mother that you wouldn't be getting your license for at least six months, but in the meantime, you'll be able to ride the bikes around here."

Marcus and Pablo let out enormous smiles. They both ran into the house to find their mother. Once they found her, they both gave her a huge hug and thanked her for letting them keep the bikes. "We love you, Momma."

She smiled and tried not to let out her fear. "I love you too, sons. Now, go get washed up for lunch."

George decided to leave the bikes in the back of the truck until the next day. Then he would unload them with the boys and give them a few pointers. He looked forward to teaching them to ride. He went back inside. He could smell lunch cooking. The aroma made his stomach growl. He tossed his hat down in the corner and kicked off his boots. George could still hear the excitement in the boys' voices.

The day went by slowly. George and Rosalia felt the boys' anticipation of having the bikes; however, there were chores to be done and other tasks around the farm.

That night George told the boys before they headed to bed that they would need to get up extra early to help unload the bikes. He wouldn't wake Rosalia in the morning. She wasn't able to sleep in too often, and it would do her good to get some extra rest.

George turned in just after dusk, because he would need an early start in the morning. More than anything, he wanted to join Rosalia in her bed, but instead he lay in bed thinking about the kiss earlier that day.

chapter

14

MARCUS AND PABLO ARRANGED the wooden boards on the tailgate of the truck. It would be tricky getting them down, but the three of them would manage. George stood in the back of the pickup and guided one of the bikes down the plank. The boys grabbed either side of the bike and helped roll it slowly to the ground. Pablo then pushed it to the side and put the kickstand down. "One down!"

"Shhh, Pablo. We want your momma to sleep for awhile," George said. Then they guided the other bike down. It went smoothly. George loaded the boards back into the truck and closed the tailgate. "Now that we have the bikes off, I want to show you boys some things before you ride them," George said. He helped the boys push the bikes down towards the barn where it would be quieter. He instructed them on how to turn the bikes on, use the clutch, throttle, and the brakes.

"Now, you boys can ride the bikes around the farm, but under no circumstances are you to go out to the road," he said. "I expect you both to abide by this rule, or I will have to take drastic measures and ban you from the bikes. I know you don't want me to do that." George sounded stern. The boys knew he meant it.

"Your momma is very worried about you boys riding motorcycles. She has every right to. So please, don't disappoint me," he added.

George then tossed each of the boys a set of keys.

"There are spare helmets in the barn, use them," he said. The boys smiled at each other. This was the best day of their life.

Later in the afternoon, the boys had been out in the barn admiring their bikes. They still couldn't believe that they finally owned their own. Pablo glanced at his watch. It was almost dinnertime. "Well, Marcus, we better head inside."

Marcus didn't want to leave the barn either but knew if they didn't, their momma would start hollering.

"Pablo?" Rosalia said as she heard the back door slam. She was in the sitting room folding laundry.

"Yes, Momma?" Pablo and Marcus entered the room with guilty expressions.

"What have you two been doing?"

"Chores, Momma," Pablo said abruptly.

"I see. Are they all done?" Rosalia looked at them with a somewhat stern look. They knew she was serious when she glared at them like that.

"Sure," Pablo said.

Marcus moved over beside Pablo.

"Momma, we still need to wash out some barrels," said Marcus.

Pablo glanced over at him. He had just told her they had finished their chores. He looked up at the ceiling as if to say 'thanks Marcus, now we're gonna get it.'

Rosalia lifted up the basket of laundry and handed it to Pablo. "Here, after dinner, you can put these clothes away. Marcus can do the barrels."

"Sure, Momma," Pablo said.

George followed them into the house, and they all sat down to enjoy the evening meal. The boys chatted up a storm about the bikes. Rosalia didn't want to hear it, but she couldn't help but be happy for them. After dinner, Pablo went into the sitting room to get the laundry to put away. Marcus dawdled and picked at his food. "Come on Marcus, eat up. You have chores to do," his momma said.

Marcus dropped his fork on his plate and huffed towards the

back door. "Why does he always get the easy chores?" As he opened the door, he looked back over his shoulder at his momma. All he heard was his momma say, "Marcus ...," in a long-winded sigh. He closed the door behind him and thumped down the steps. Once he got to the bottom step, he plunked down on his ass. He sat there with his elbows on his knees, and held his face in his hands. A few minutes went by until he finally bolted up off the stairs and ran to the barn. He didn't bother to see if anyone was looking or not. Once in the barn, he headed over to where he had covered up the bottle of whiskey. *This should cure everything,* he thought. He twisted the cap off and smelled the contents. "Oh my gawd! This stinks!"

He remembered what his momma always told him to do if something stunk and he didn't like the taste. He'd always seen others drink it straight out of the bottle, and it never seemed to hurt them. He plugged his nose tightly and put the bottle to his mouth. He felt the cool liquid hit his lips and then his tongue, but he lifted the bottle up more than he had realized. His mouth suddenly filled with whiskey. He tried to swallow but couldn't because his nose was plugged, so he unplugged it. The moment he let go of his nose, was when he got his first taste of the nastiest flavour he had ever tasted. It burned all the way down his throat. Marcus felt like it wasn't going to stay down. He started to violently gag and cough, and his stomach was retching. He held his throat for dear life. The bottle had fallen from his hands onto the barn floor, luckily it didn't break. Marcus noticed he had dropped it and quickly recovered it before the contents seeped out. He stood it up, and then he fell against one of the stalls near the back of the barn. He leaned against it, trying to catch his breath. Once he was in control again, he took in a deep breath. His throat still burned. He wondered how long it would last. He slid his back down the wall and sat on the floor, his legs bent in front of him. He rested his head on his knees. He felt like shit. Marcus glanced over at the bottle. He had to have swallowed two ounces in one shot. He shook his head. He wondered why others never made any gestures when they drank the stuff. Marcus didn't understand. A few moments later, he started to feel warm all over. He didn't want to move now. A smile crossed his face. It seemed to be automatic. Marcus hardly ever smiled when alone. *This is weird*, he thought.

Pablo wandered out to the back porch after he'd put the laundry away. George was lying back in the chair and had his hat tilted forward on his head, as if he was taking a nap. Pablo sat down on the wooden chair beside him. It creaked as he settled. George lifted the brim of his hat and glanced over at Pablo.

"Hey, George," Pablo said.

George lifted himself up on the chair. "Hey, Pab. Did you get your bike out?"

"No, not yet. Marcus isn't finished doing the barrels. I wish he would hurry. It will be dark in a couple of hours."

There was silence between them for a bit before Pablo got up the nerve to ask George some questions. He really didn't have anything to lose now that they had made that mess in the barn.

"George? Do you know anything about what's under the crate in the barn?" Pablo asked.

George looked sharply at Pablo. "What do you mean?"

"The crate, there's a door underneath. Do you know what's down there?"

"How do you know about that?" George asked quietly. "Move your chair over here a bit."

Pablo moved closer to his uncle.

"Now listen, Pablo, you mustn't repeat any of this to your momma or Marcus. It would drive her over the edge, and Marcus doesn't need to know. I think you can handle what I have to tell you."

"It was an accident. I swear!" Pablo said worriedly, thinking his uncle knew that the crate had fallen.

"Accident? Where?" George said suddenly, not knowing what Pablo was talking about.

Pablo was trying to get everything out at once and none of it was making sense to his uncle.

"Calm down, Pablo. Now tell me, what exactly *are* you talking about?"

Pablo took a deep breath. "The crate, the trapdoor ... it fell right through to the bottom!"

"Oh shit, really? You know, I told your dad time and time again, that the barn should be rebuilt. The wood in that barn is so dry and brittle, but your dad would never listen to a word I said. It wasn't your fault it fell, Pablo. It was bound to sooner or later. Don't worry about it. I'll fix it when I'm out there."

Pablo looked at his uncle. *His uncle knew? Then it must be his stuff,* he thought. He braced himself as to what else George might tell him. Pablo sat back in the chair and tried not to burst out again. He asked calmly, as if he didn't know, "What's down there?"

"Well," George said, carefully collecting his thoughts, "I store some personal stuff there that I don't want stolen. I would keep them in the farmhouse, but it's not secure enough. Know what I mean?"

"Well, I guess." Pablo was hoping George would go into more detail. He waited patiently, and then said, "So, what *kind* of things are down there?"

George was hesitant to tell Pablo exactly what was down there, so he tried to avoid some of his questions by changing the subject. He casually lit a cigarette.

"So, how about we get those bikes out tomorrow?"

Pablo stared at his uncle. *Why was he avoiding the question?* he wondered. Pablo wasn't going to stop asking them now. He needed to know. "Uncle George ..."

"Yes?" George braced himself.

"I found a book down there."

"A book?" George tried to sound surprised. "What book?"

"It's called 'Riders of Reason.'"

George figured that there was no sense in lying to the boy, and really, what would it hurt? "That's my book, son."

"I've read some of it, and it looks like it belongs to a motorcycle gang. Are you in a gang, Uncle George?"

"Well, I wouldn't say a gang so-to-speak, but a club, yes." There was a brief pause. "Okay, yes, it is more like a gang than a 'club' that one would belong to generally."

Pablo was confused. "So you *do* belong to a gang?" He stood up quickly as if he was in shock.

George took Pablo's hand and gently pulled him back down to a sitting position. "Pablo, you mustn't say anything to anyone about this. You have to promise me. It's very important that you don't read into this book too much."

Pablo stared at his uncle. "What do you mean, Uncle George?"

George tossed his butt into the dirt. "Well son, it hasn't been a pleasant trip with this club. I would like more than anything to tell you, but personally, I would rather you just forget about it. As a matter of fact, I am no longer with them."

"Oh, why not?" Pablo asked with interest.

"It's a long story, Pab, and I can't tell you right now."

"Is it true Uncle George, that you had to sign an oath? I mean ... why do you have to sign one?"

"Yes, it's part of becoming a full member," George said. He wasn't going to go into detail about the patches and what he really had to do in the club.

"What does it mean, once it's signed?" Pablo was not letting up on the questions as George had wished.

"It just means that you belong ... and you will be loyal ... you know, like you would not belong to another motorcycle club." George lied a bit and hoped this would be enough to steer Pablo in another direction.

"So why aren't you with them anymore?"

George looked away, towards the barn.

"It was just taking up too much of my time, and since your dad is away working away a lot, I felt that I should be here for you boys and your mom."

Pablo had no reason *not* to believe his uncle.

"Please keep this information and the book away from Marcus," George added. "He's easily influenced."

"Okay, Uncle George, I will do my best. But he has seen it and knows I have it," said Pablo.

"Well, see what you can do. Maybe bring it downstairs to me and I'll dispose of it."

Pablo had a feeling there was more to this club than his uncle was saying. He would do his best to keep the book and read it before his uncle wanted it back.

"Okay George. You don't mind if I keep it for a bit, do you?"

"Sure, but the longer you keep it, the more chances are that Marcus will want to read it." George put his arm around Pablo and gave him a squeeze.

"I-I-I promise," Pablo said hesitantly. "Do you think sometime we can sit down together and look through it?"

George wasn't keen on how persistent Pablo had become about the book. He would now have to sidetrack him with other things to try to keep his mind off of it. The last thing the boys needed was to know too much about 'Riders of Reason.'

Pablo had a lot to think about. "George, is that where you disappeared all the time?"

"Yes."

"Is it dangerous?"

"Yes son, more dangerous than you realize." George turned his head away and lit up another cigarette.

Pablo could sense his uncle had had enough questioning for now. He got up off the chair and walked to the edge of the porch. He looked towards the barrels at the side of the building where Marcus and he had left them. He glanced back at George.

"Have you seen Marcus? He's supposed to be over there," Pablo said as he pointed at the barrels.

"He ran past me a while ago, towards the barn, I think. I'm not for certain though, as I was dozing off and on."

The barn? Pablo thought. *Hmmm, what's he up to now?*

George shook his head. "Maybe you should go check on him."

It didn't take much to talk Pablo into doing just that. He rushed off the porch and sprinted to the barn. The barn door was partly open. Pablo didn't want to startle Marcus, so he quietly slid inside. He stood in the dark for a moment to get his bearings, and if he could hear anything. There was no noise except for a slight rustling of the hay in the far corner. *Might be a mouse*, he thought. And there was a funny odour; smelled like ... booze! He walked carefully towards the sound. Just as he rounded the corner of one of the stalls, he saw Marcus huddled against the wall. Pablo bent down to see if he was sleeping. Marcus' eyes were closed and his hand was wrapped around a bottle. Pablo reached down and slid the bottle out of his hand. *You little shit!* Pablo let out a slight chuckle. He raised the bottle towards the window to see how much was in it. *Barely a mouthful. You're gonna be one sick puppy when you wake up.* He propped Marcus up so that he wouldn't fall over. "Luckily it's not winter, or you'd freeze your balls off out here," Pablo said.

Pablo stood up and removed his flannel shirt. He placed it over Marcus. "This should keep you warm." Pablo wasn't so sure leaving him in the barn with that hole in the floor was a good idea. He would talk to his uncle and find out what he should do with Marcus, or if he should just leave him in the barn. He hoped he would be okay until he returned. He moved away from Marcus, and so he wouldn't wake him, he quietly walked out of the barn.

Once out, he raced to the back porch. George had already gone inside. "Damn." Pablo opened the back door and went to find his uncle. He rushed into the kitchen. His momma was doing up the dinner dishes and humming away. She seemed to be in a rather pleasant mood, which was odd when their dad wasn't home.

Maybe it was because George was home, Pablo thought. It was nice to see. "Momma, where's George?" Pablo asked.

Rosalia turned towards him. "He's getting washed up, son. He'll be out shortly."

"Okay."

"Everything alright?"

"Sure, everything's fine."

"Where's Marcus?"

"Just outside, getting some air."

"Well, you boys outta get in soon before the dew hits or you'll be down with a cold."

Pablo nodded. "Yup, we'll be in soon." Pablo wasn't sure how he was going to talk to his uncle now with his momma in the kitchen. *Think, Pablo, think.* If he didn't go back out and get Marcus, his momma would start questioning him. Pablo left the kitchen and went into the sitting room. He sat on the far side of the sofa, in the dark. His uncle would have to pass by him to go to his room. *Hopefully, this will work*, he thought.

Pablo waited for about ten minutes before his uncle finally made an appearance in the sitting room. "P-s-s-st," Pablo said quietly. "Don't turn the light on."

George stood still. "Pab? What's up?"

"Just stay there, I'll come to you." Pablo went to where his uncle was. "Okay, listen, we have a problem outside."

"What kind of problem?"

"Meet me out on the back porch." Pablo left the room and headed out through the kitchen.

"What, you haven't gone to get Marcus yet?" his momma said. She was now sitting at the kitchen table sipping a cup of tea.

"Heading there now, Momma." Pablo hurried out the back door before she could say anything else. Seconds later, George entered the kitchen.

"I thought you retired for the night?" Rosalia looked up at him with a slight smile.

"Yes, I started to, but then realized I hadn't had my last cigarette for the night. You know if I don't have one before I crash, I'll be up in the middle of the night stumbling around to go have one." As George walked past Rosalia, he gently squeezed her shoulders. She briefly shut her eyes. His touch made her feel warm all over.

"Well, you just be cautious out there. Those wooden slats are slippery when they're damp," she said. George smiled at her as he opened the back door. Carefully, he closed it behind him.

Rosalia shivered. *It is chilly tonight*, she thought.

"Okay, Pab, make this quick," George said as he stood there lighting up a cigarette.

"Marcus is passed out in the barn," Pablo said hurriedly.

"Passed out? He didn't look that tired earlier," George said.

"No, I said passed out! You know——pissed——drunk!"

"What? How?" George knew that Rosalia didn't allow alcohol around the boys, or in the house.

"I-I-I don't know," Pablo said. "But there's an empty whiskey bottle in the barn. It was in his hand, but I took it."

George chuckled. "Oh my Lord, what is your momma gonna say?!"

"She can't find out!" Pablo said quietly. "Hey, you made me keep a secret, now it's your turn!"

George liked the quick response from Pablo. He was a bright young man. "Yes, yes I did. Okay, I'll do my best." George gritted his teeth trying to hold back his smirk. "What do we do with Marcus if he's passed out?"

"I was thinking we could leave him there, but he may fall into that hole where the crate fell down," Pablo said.

"Oh yes, the crate," George said. "We will have to wait until your momma goes to bed, but that might not be for a while."

"Okay, then you can cover for us both," Pablo said. "I'm going to stay with him in the barn tonight to make sure he's alright."

"What am I going to tell your momma?" George asked.

Pablo gave it some thought. "You will have to stay up until she goes to bed."

George sighed. He was tired and wasn't sure he could stay up much longer. "Okay, son. I'll do my best to cover for both of you. Are you going to be warm enough out there?"

"We'll need a blanket," Pablo said. "Can you leave one for us on the porch? I can come and get it when the lights are out."

"Sure. Now you get out there with Marcus. I don't want to see you until morning."

George suddenly thought, *Whiskey? Crate, barn? Oh shit, that was my whiskey!*

Pablo thanked his uncle and gave him a hug. "I wish you were our dad." He ran back to the barn to be with Marcus.

George watched as Pablo entered the barn and closed the door. *Damn kids.* He went into the farmhouse and made his way into the sitting room, but he didn't see Rosalia. *This would be a good time to grab a blanket for the boys,* he thought. He went into his room and pulled one of the blankets off of his bed. He went back outside, put the blanket on the chair by the door, and then went back in. He hoped the boys would be warm enough. George knew Marcus wouldn't feel the cold with all the alcohol in his blood.

Rosalia came out of the bathroom with her robe wrapped loosely around her. "You're still up?"

"Yes, I wasn't as tired as I thought," George replied. "Oh, and the boys are already upstairs." He didn't like lying to Rosalia, but he did make a promise to Pablo.

Rosalia turned her head to listen. "It sure is quiet up there, isn't it?"

"Yes, they seemed to be pretty burned out."

"Well, it has been a busy couple of weeks for them," she replied. "I'm gonna go say goodnight to the boys."

"Ah, no. They're probably already asleep." George put a hand on her arm, and squeezed gently.

Rosalia looked into his eyes. "Well, okay. I guess I better turn in then." She didn't want to move his hand away.

"Okay, Rosa. I think I'll try too." George let go of her arm. "You go ahead. Sleep well." He waited until she was in her room before he turned off the lights. He left his door ajar, so he could hear the boys if they came in during the night.

Pablo was huddled near Marcus for about an hour. He was shivering so bad that he got up to go see if his uncle had left a blanket for them. Luckily he had. Pablo wrapped it around both Marcus and himself. It was going to be a long night.

chapter

15

MARCUS FELT LIKE HIS STOMACH was in his throat. He leaned forward and vomited all over the floorboards in front of him. This woke Pablo. He quickly moved out of the way and helped hold Marcus up. "You okay, Marcus?"

Marcus looked up at him, but as he did, he turned away quickly as his stomach heaved again. Pablo rubbed his back, trying to comfort him. "It'll be okay."

Marcus was almost in tears. *Why did I drink that whiskey?*

It took about forty minutes before his stomach stopped heaving. Once Pablo knew it was clear, he helped Marcus sit back against the wall. Marcus was grateful for his brother. He didn't know what he would have done without him. He closed his eyes, and before he knew it, he had passed out. Pablo made sure Marcus was in a sitting position and not lying down, just in case he got sick again. He glanced up at the window and could see the silhouette of the moon. It was around 1:00 in the morning, and the boys were going to be exhausted when they got up. Pablo leaned against Marcus and closed his eyes.

Pablo woke up around 5:00 A.M. His back and neck were so stiff from the cold and the position he had slept in. Marcus had fallen onto his side and was still asleep. Pablo would have to wake him up and get him into the house before their momma woke up. He reached over and shook Marcus lightly. "Hey, bro." Marcus fidgeted a little. Pablo shook him. "Marcus, come on. You gotta get up."

Marcus turned to look up at Pablo. Marcus looked lost, as if he didn't know where he was. It took a minute for it to sink in that he was in the barn.

"You okay?" Pablo asked.

"Uh huh. I think so," Marcus said. He pushed himself up into a sitting position and looked around. "How'd we get in here?"

"Don't you remember last night?" Pablo asked.

"No." Marcus moved his hand down to his stomach. "But I feel really sick." Marcus noticed the mess on the floor in front of him. Then he started to remember. "I guess I was sick last night?"

"Yes, very sick, Marcus. Come on. Let's get in the house before Momma finds out. You're gonna need to drink lots of water!"

"Okay."

Pablo helped Marcus stand up and guided him out of the barn towards the house.

"Much better out here," Marcus said, as he breathed in the fresh cool air.

Pablo looked up at the porch and saw his uncle standing there.

Marcus noticed as well. "Shit, now we're gonna get it."

"Don't worry, Marcus, he's on our side."

"Really?" Marcus said.

"Yup, come on."

"He's not well, George," Pablo said, as they walked past George on their way into the house.

"I can see that," George said. "Best take him right up to his room. I'll try to convince your momma not to wake you boys. Go get some rest."

"Thanks Uncle George," Marcus said under his breath. The boys went as quietly as they could to their room. Pablo closed the door and helped Marcus into bed. "Don't worry about undressing, just get in," Pablo said.

Pablo covered Marcus up with the quilt and closed the curtains to hide the daylight. Then he jumped into his bed and hid under the blankets. It didn't take long before the boys were sound asleep.

George sat at the kitchen table nursing a hot cup of instant coffee when Rosalia came in.

"Good morning, sunshine," he said.

She blushed and said good morning.

"I hope you slept well?" George said.

"Yes, as a matter of fact, I was out like a light, and didn't hear anything all night. I was amazed I slept so well, considering ..."

"That's great," George said. "I haven't perked any coffee yet, but there's some hot water on the stove if you would like some instant coffee."

"Thanks, George. Any sign of the boys? It seems they are late rising as well."

"Well, Rosa, I was thinking ..." There was a pause. "Maybe we should let them sleep as long as they want today. I know they have chores, but they have also been going through a lot the last little while. What do you think?"

Rosalia poured some boiling water into her cup and a teaspoon of instant coffee. She stirred it slowly and looked over at George. "Sure. I agree." She was hesitant but knew it was a good idea. She walked over to the table and sat down across from George.

It was 8:00 A.M., and Pablo lay on his bed wide awake. He wasn't able to sleep any longer. Thoughts went through his head at what his Uncle George had told him about the book the night before.

Pablo leaned over and pulled the book out from under his mattress. He quietly thumbed through the pages. He didn't want to wake up Marcus. He didn't understand why George didn't want Marcus to know about his belonging to the motorcycle club, yet he had told him. *Why was he protecting Marcus*, he wondered. The photos in the book showed pictures of members all across the USA, as well as Canada; the club appeared to be worldwide. Pablo hadn't realized how big the club really was. *Wow*. It was like one big family. *Why did his uncle join in the first place?*

Marcus stirred a bit. He rolled over onto his side and then held his stomach. It hurt like hell; he knew he wasn't going to drink that stuff again anytime soon.

Rosalia headed up the ladder to the loft. She knocked lightly on the door. Pablo kept quiet and slid the book under his blanket. He lay down on his pillow and closed his eyes. Shortly after, the door opened a bit and Rosalia peeked in. She was shocked that they were both still asleep. She said quietly, "Boys? It's getting late." She waited for them to stir. The room had an odd odour to it.

A few seconds later, Pablo opened his eyes. "Momma." He rubbed his eyes, as if he'd just woken up. "What time is it?"

"It is almost 9:00. I thought I would let you boys sleep in today, but I can't let you sleep all day or the chores won't get done."

"Thanks, Momma. I'll wake Marcus and we'll be down in a few minutes."

"Okay, son." She closed the door behind her and went back down to the kitchen.

Pablo crawled out of his bed and wandered over to Marcus' bed. "Marcus," he said quietly. "Marcus?"

Marcus stirred a bit and then opened his eyes.

"How are you feeling?" Pablo asked.

"Like shit," Marcus moved his hand to his head. "My head hurts so much."

"I can imagine," Pablo said. "Next time you do something like you did last night, I may not be around to help you out."

"Yeah, I know. Thanks." Marcus turned over onto his side and made himself get out of bed. "I have a feeling I won't be doing that again." He held his stomach tightly. "How does anyone drink that stuff so easily?"

"Well, probably because they're used to it," Pablo said, "and maybe they didn't drink almost a full bottle!" He grinned.

"I sure don't want to get used to it."

"We should make an appearance downstairs," Pablo said. "Try not to whine too much, okay. I don't want to have to explain this to anyone. Maybe change your clothes and brush your teeth."

Marcus nodded. He noticed he was still dressed from the night before. "Tell Momma I'll be right there."

Pablo headed downstairs to the kitchen to where his momma and Uncle George were sitting.

"Where's Marcus?" Momma said.

"He's coming."

"Coffee?" George asked.

"You bet," Pablo said. Marcus walked into the kitchen shortly after, right past the kitchen table and into the bathroom. He looked back at Pablo. He washed up and sat down across from his uncle, while Rosalia poured him some coffee.

"How was your night?" George asked Marcus. George had a slight grin on his face.

"Fine," Marcus said.

"That's great. I hope you boys caught up on some needed sleep," George said.

"I have to head into town and pick up some groceries," Rosalia told the boys. "I'll be back in a couple of hours. Maybe you two should think of doing up your chores before anything else."

The boys nodded, as they watched her leave the room.

"Don't worry, Rosa, I'll make sure they get them done," George hollered before she went out the front door.

"So, what's in the plans today?" The boys looked like they hadn't slept in days.

Pablo glanced up at him. "Not sure yet."

George looked over at Marcus. "You didn't have a very good night, did you? I believe you might have a mess to clean up in the barn, as well?"

Marcus looked over at Pablo.

"I'll help you," Pablo cut in.

George got up. "I'll come out when you boys are done and fix that hole in the floor before your dad comes home. Marcus, take a couple of aspirins. You're young—you'll be fine. And eat something!"

The boys sat across from each other nursing their coffee. It wasn't going down very well for Marcus, so he pushed it away.

"Let's go out and clean up the barn." Pablo rose from his chair and grabbed Marcus' arm. "Come on." Marcus didn't have much choice but to follow Pablo.

"Don't worry, you'll feel better in a few hours," Pablo said. "It does go away."

"Thankfully!" Marcus said under his breath. He felt like he had the worst flu ever.

It took the boys an hour to clean up the barn. Marcus tried to keep himself busy, so that he wouldn't think about how awful he felt. Pablo tossed him the empty bottle. "Here, get rid of it."

Marcus caught it and put it in the garbage bin. They stood over the hole in the floor.

"Sure hope Dad doesn't know we did this," Pablo said. He leaned up against a stall and had a piece of hay sticking out of his mouth. "Marcus, I have to tell you something."

"Sure, what?"

"Well, the stuff we found down there isn't Dad's, it's Uncle George's, and he belongs to a motorcycle club; it's not a good one," Pablo explained.

"Oh? But what about Dad? I mean, he disappears all the time too, and that might have been him in the photo. Where else does he go?" Marcus asked.

"Not sure, maybe Uncle George will be able to answer some of our questions, now that he'll be home for a while," Pablo added.

"I hope so," Marcus said.

Bernardo had come home late in the afternoon that day, while the boys were out doing their chores. They had no idea he was back.

Rosalia had returned to the farmhouse to start dinner for Bernardo, George and the boys. She turned towards her husband.

"I haven't heard from the boys in a while," she said, "have you?"

Bernardo thought. "As a matter a fact, no, I haven't seen them either. Not since I've been home."

"That's odd. They're usually in and out most of the day," she said. "Maybe they're on their bikes?"

"Bikes?"

"Oh, you don't know ..." Rosalia had briefly forgotten that Bernardo had no idea the boys had motorcycles.

He looked at Rosalia sharply. "What? What did you just say?"

Rosalia thought she might as well get it out. It would be best this way, as it had been stressing her out quite a bit.

"George took the boys out and helped them buy motorcycles. It wasn't his ..."

Bernardo interrupted her before she could finish. "Did he now? I can't believe he would do that, after all ..." He stopped talking.

"After all what?" Rosalia asked with concern in her voice.

"Nothing."

"Please don't hide things from me!" she said.

"I'm ... not. Look, maybe you should go check on the boys."

Rosalia sat down. *What had she done? What would George think of her now?* She was worried for him and the boys.

Bernardo suddenly got up and went out to the back porch. He didn't know how he was going to tackle his sons about the bikes, and he was not impressed with George or Rosalia. He would have to sit George down and have a talk with him. He felt his brother was interfering with his family too much now, and making decisions that were not his to make. It made Bernardo feel more guilty that he was absent so damn much. He also wondered what else might be going on that he didn't know about.

George had gone out to the barn before the boys had finished cleaning the mess Marcus had made the night before. He had them hold the pieces of the trapdoor together while he affixed other boards across it. Once they had it positioned on the floor, George had the boys pile some hay on top of it. They didn't put the crate back over it or it would just fall through again.

"Thanks, Uncle George," Pablo said. "I hope Dad doesn't notice."

"I don't think he will, Pablo, at least not right away," George said. You boys best check in with your momma. The boys agreed and raced back to the farmhouse, but as they neared the top of the stairs, they heard a husky voice in the far corner of the porch. Startled, the boys turned towards the voice. They stood there, staring at their dad, who had his legs propped up the edge of the railing. The boys stayed silent, as if they had never seen him before.

Bernardo repeated what he had said, "What are ya boys running from? You look like you'd seen a ghost."

Marcus wanted to run inside; he didn't want to do any explaining, but Pablo grabbed the back of his arm and pulled him closer, as if to say, you're not going anywhere.

Pablo spoke up, "We were——" He had to think carefully. He turned his head towards the barn. "We were ... doing chores." He nudged Marcus.

Bernardo knew they were hiding something. Pablo didn't sound convincing enough, and he wasn't good at telling lies. Marcus on the other hand, was sneakier, and his dad would sometimes have to second-guess whether he was telling the truth. "Marcus, you look frightened. Are you sure you're okay?" their dad asked.

Marcus looked over at Pablo and back at his dad. "Yeah." He hung his head and started kicking a piece of wood that was lifting on the floor of the porch. Bernardo wasn't going to press them any further, but he would get the truth out of them one way or the other.

"Go on then."

That evening it was very quiet in the Gomez's farmhouse. It was unbearable for Rosalia, so she went into the kitchen to keep herself busy. The boys had already retired for the night. It was early yet, but the boys could sense something wasn't right.

"Hey Pablo, Dad seems mighty pissed, don't you think?" Marcus said.

Pablo looked up from what he was doing. "Yeah, I think he is. I have a feeling it's about the bikes, Marcus. You know he never wanted us to have any."

"Yeah, I know. Shit, Pab, we're old enough! Even Uncle George says we are."

"Don't worry so much, Marcus. I'm sure things will be fine." Pablo always tried to make Marcus feel less stressed about things, even though he felt the same way.

There was a sudden commotion downstairs and Pablo waved at Marcus to follow him. The boys sneaked out of their room and into the hallway. The floorboards creaked slightly. They both positioned themselves onto their stomachs on the floor and laid their heads down. They could hear better this way.

"Damn it, George, how could you?!" Bernardo hollered.

George sat quietly on the edge of the sofa. He knew Bernardo was going to be upset but not to this extreme. "Listen Bernardo, the boys have proven themselves to be responsible ..." George tried to hold his cool for as long as possible.

Bernardo impatiently paced the floor. He was ready to hurt someone. The last thing he ever wanted was for the boys to own motorcycles. He stopped and glared at George and then shook his head. The overwhelming feeling he was experiencing was not pleasant.

"Not the boys, George! We've talked about this many times. The boys were not t——" Then there was silence. "We need to talk, privately——outside!"

George got up and followed Bernardo out to the back porch. The door slammed behind them. Rosalia shuddered as the door settled into the jam. She tossed the tea towel onto the sink and went into her bedroom.

Marcus and Pablo got up off the floor and rushed back into their room. Their room faced the front of the house, so they weren't able to hear what George and their dad were saying.

"Pablo, what's going on?"

"I'm not sure, Marcus."

Bernardo walked down the back steps and towards the field. He didn't want anyone else to hear what he was going to say to George. George followed like an obedient puppy. He knew he wronged Bernardo, but at the same time, he hoped he was helping the boys mature into men. They continued walking until they reached the run-down shed. Bernardo cornered George inside. "Look, I didn't want to say anything inside so that the boys would hear, but I want you to leave the farm. I can't trust you anymore." Bernardo pulled out a cigarette and lit it.

"What? Bernardo, are you sure?" George was in shock. Never did he think that Bernardo would ask him to leave the farm ... the boys ... and Rosalia!

"Yes, I am fucking sure!"

"Look, can we talk about this?" George was hoping Bernardo and he would come to an agreement.

"No! I've made up my mind. I expect you to be gone before I get back," Bernardo said. "It's one thing that *you* are involved with motorcycles, but when you start bringing my sons into it——that's where I draw the line!"

"What do you mean before you get back? You just got home!" George tried to avoid what Bernardo said, because he hoped Bernardo was just blowing off steam.

Bernardo wasn't going to listen to anymore of what George had to say. He tossed his butt onto the floor of the shed and stepped on it on his way out. He turned his head back towards George and said, "No one's to know!"

George stood there at the doorway of the shed watching Bernardo. "Know? Know what ...?" It was as if Bernardo was hiding something.

Bernardo continued walking, ignoring George. George went back into the shed and sat on a bucket for a few minutes trying to soak in what just happened. *There must be something going on with him*, he thought. *But what?*

Bernardo walked into the farmhouse. The boys were in the kitchen.

"Dad, what's up?" Pablo asked.

"Nothing," he said, and he kicked his boots off.

"I thought I heard ..." Pablo started to say.

"You heard nothing, son! You two, get to bed!"

Before Marcus opened his mouth to say something he might regret, Pablo grabbed his arm and they headed to the loft.

Bernardo emptied the contents of the boys' cups into the sink. They had been in the middle of making iced-tea when he stormed into the house. "Fuck 'em all!" he said. He was so tired of the shit he had to deal with day in and day out. He had wished he could just stay home and nurture his family properly, like a real dad. Now, he has asked the only role model the boys had in their life to leave. Bernardo didn't feel good about his decision, but he had to stand by what he believed in. He could be as stubborn as a mule, but right now, he was confused, angry and afraid of losing Rosalia.

chapter

16

GEORGE DECIDED TO WAIT a while before he went back into the house. He knew by then the dust would have settled, or least he hoped it would have.

Rosalia was sitting quietly in the dark when Bernardo entered the bedroom. He noticed her shadow in the window. *How was he going to tell her?* He decided he wouldn't. This could be the last time he would see her for quite some time. He walked over to her and placed his hands on her shoulders. She leaned her head back. She missed his touch. Bernardo bent down and kissed the top of her head. "You okay?" he asked.

Rosalia moved her hand up to his and squeezed it. "Yes, I'm fine, just tired."

"How about we call it a night?"

Rosalia stood up and found herself in Bernardo's embrace. He kissed her deeply. He moved her towards the bed until they were both lying down next to each other. He ran his hands up and down her soft skin. Rosalia melted in his arms.

Bernardo left a note next to the coffee pot the next morning. He figured it would be the best way to say 'good-bye,' instead of face-to-face. He knew he wouldn't be able to handle the tears, not again. He left the house quietly so as not to disturb anyone.

Rosalia woke around 6:00 A.M., much later than her usual time. She reached over to find Bernardo's side of the bed cold and empty. She quickly got up and ran out to the sitting room. She looked out the window and noticed his truck was gone. She gasped. *No, he couldn't have left already.* Rosalia went into the kitchen and found the note. She read it carefully, but not without tears.

Rosalia, my dear, I must leave again. I am sorry it's so sudden, but something came up during the night. I apologize. You and the boys are my world. Please take good care of them. Love Bernardo.

Rosalia quickly scrunched the note up and tucked it in the pocket of her robe. She didn't want anyone to see it. She ran into the bathroom and slammed the door. George had heard the noise, so he got up out of bed, pulled on his boxers and went to the kitchen. "Rosa? Rosa? Are you okay?" He pressed his ear against the bathroom door.

Rosalia stood against the sink sobbing uncontrollably. Bernardo had never left a note for her before, so she knew, deep down, that he was gone for a long time. She gasped for a breath. She wanted to answer George but couldn't find the strength.

George tried the door handle; it was unlocked. He gently turned it and peeked in. "Rosa?"

She turned to look at him. She couldn't tell him about the note; it wouldn't be fair to involve him. "George, yes I'm fine ... really." She tried to get a grip, blew her nose, and then straightened herself up. She had to keep herself together for the boys.

George walked behind her and placed his arms around her waist. He held her close. He tried his hardest not to show his real feelings towards her but found it very difficult. How was he going to tell her that he had to leave the farm? He figured he would wait until after lunch. "Where's Bernardo?"

"Bernardo ... oh, um, he had to go out this morning."

"Why the tears?"

"I'm not sure. I think I'm just emotional right now." She pushed him back a bit and took a deep breath. "So, what would you like for breakfast?"

George thought, *My damn brother! How can he leave this fine woman and the boys——they needed him.*

"Breakfast? Hey, tell you what ... how about I cook you breakfast this morning?" George suggested. It had been a while since he had cooked anything.

"You?" Rosalia laughed.

At least George got a chuckle out of her. "Yes me." He liked it when she laughed; her smile could light up any room, even in the dark.

"Well, sure then. Is there anything I can do?"

"Nope, I have it under control. You just have a seat, and I'll be your servant today."

"But we won't get any cooking done in here!" She laughed again. They walked into the kitchen.

Rosalia liked his idea and she was amazed it had taken her mind off Bernardo, if only for a moment. She reached down to her pocket to make sure the note had stayed inside. She poured some coffee.

"Listen Rosa, I need to tell you something." George was hesitant but knew he had to tell her. He couldn't just get up and leave with no explanation.

"Sure, George." She listened intently.

"Last night Bernardo asked me to leave the farm." George had hoped to let it out more gently but couldn't find the right words.

"What!?" Rosalia sat down. "He asked you to ... what?"

"He asked me to leave. He really didn't explain anything, but I have a feeling it's because I helped the boys buy the bikes."

"But ... but, you can't leave, George!" She was getting upset. More upset than George had expected. George placed his arm around her to comfort her.

"George, you can't go!" She stared into his eyes.

George moved his hand up to wipe the tears that were streaming down her face.

"When? When are you leaving?"

"Well, he wants me gone by the time he gets home. And if he's only out for a bit, then I should probably get my things and leave."

Rosalia couldn't believe what was happening to her life; it was crumbling down all around her. "I can't believe he asked you to leave!"

The boys had heard their momma crying from upstairs and came running into the kitchen. "Momma? What's wrong?" Pablo said. He found his Uncle George sitting next to her, holding her close.

George felt there was no sense in hiding anything from the boys. They were old enough to know what was going on. "Listen, Pab, I have to go."

"Go? Go where? I thought you were staying for a while?"

"No, son. I have to leave the farm. Your dad has asked this of me, and I will abide by his decision. Look boys, Rosa, how about we talk about this after lunch? I think we're all too upset right now to think clearly."

Rosalia nodded her head. Pablo had a lot to say but bit his tongue. The boys sat down at the kitchen table with their momma and uncle. They all stared at each other.

"Where's Dad?" Pablo suddenly asked.

Rosalia got up from the table, rushed into her bedroom and slammed the door.

Pablo sat quietly.

George looked grim, but said, "Okay. We'll talk later. I'm on breakfast duty this morning!"

The boys looked at their uncle, this was a first.

Bernardo drove for about twenty minutes before he had to pull the truck over at the next gas station. He wasn't feeling good at all about leaving Rosalia and the boys behind, and he felt rotten about George. He would arrive in Santa Isabel in a few hours, but he needed coffee. He climbed out of the truck and strolled into the station.

"Hey handsome," one of the women behind the counter said.

He glanced up and smiled. She was a pretty little thing, about five-foot-two, blonde hair down the middle of her back, which she kept tightly bound in a tight braid. She was wearing a tight-fitting, baby blue T-shirt that squeezed her chest so it rose higher than it normally would. The neckline was low and revealed the fresh, innocent flesh of a bouncy adolescent. The back of the T-shirt was higher than her slim fitting jeans that sat firmly on her hips. The opening at the back revealed a tiny tattoo on the lower part her spine. Bernardo wondered what the tattoo was, but unfortunately, he would have to get closer to see it. She was too young for him, but that never stopped him from flirting; today he wasn't feeling much like doing anything.

"Hey, are you alright cowboy?" she asked in her perky little voice.

Bernardo chuckled to himself. She had always called him 'cowboy,' and he couldn't figure out why, because he never wore a Stetson or even cowboy boots. As always, he let it go and played along with her.

"Just fine." Bernardo wandered over to the coffee machine. He placed a cup underneath the spout and pushed the button. The cup started to fill up and then stopped. "Damn, that figures."

The girl at the cash register heard him and motioned for someone to refill the coffee machine. "Someone will be right there, handsome!"

Bernardo was thankful he wasn't her age anymore, because he knew he wouldn't be able to handle the peppy young ones with all their energy. Although, he wished he could at times! He swore they had a switch in them that was wound up and then let go because it seemed like they never stopped! He paid for his coffee and returned to his truck.

Bernardo hadn't even packed clothing this time. He was in too much of a hurry to leave before Rosalia woke up. *Three more hours.* He sighed.

The sun was now up and it was glaring through his windshield, blinding him.

It's going to be a hot one. He drove around the next bend.

The morning dragged by slowly as the boys anticipated the talk they were going to have with their uncle after lunch. They would miss their uncle terribly and knew their mother would also be lost. They sat on the back steps waiting patiently until the screen door finally opened. Their uncle and momma came outside.

"Okay, sons," she said, "we need to make some decisions."

Rosalia sat down beside the boys on the step, while George leaned against the post. "Your dad is gone again. He was called away early this morning."

Pablo didn't want to talk about his dad. He was more concerned about his uncle. Pablo turned around to face George. "Where will you go?"

"I'm not sure, son." There were tears in his eyes. "You boys are my family. You're all I have." Pablo rose to his feet and submerged himself into George's chest. George held him tight. "You boys are like my own sons. I would never abandon you."

Marcus said, "Abandon? What the hell do you think you're doing?"

Rosalia hushed Marcus. Marcus always had a way of blurting things out first before thinking. She placed her hand on his knee and squeezed. "It'll be okay, Marcus."

Marcus looked at his step-mom. "Everyone keeps saying that!"

"Like I was saying, I won't abandon you boys," George said. "I will visit often, as much as I can."

The boys didn't like what was going on, but they had no say in the matter.

Rosalia took a breath and had to remain strong for the boys. She stood up. "Okay, George. I know the boys understand, but even if they don't, I know you won't abandon them, and we thank you for that."

George placed his free arm around her waist and pulled her close. "I know Rosa, and thank you for believing in me."

Early in the afternoon, George was packed and ready to leave. Pablo had told George he could take the extra work truck and that if they needed it they would call. George appreciated that because he didn't have a vehicle. The boys said their 'good-byes' and George went out to the truck. Rosalia followed him, carrying another bag. The boys stood on the front porch. They knew George would be back; it would just be a matter of time. After George was in the truck, he closed the door and rolled down the window. Rosalia stood there quietly. He would miss her just as much. Rosalia patted his arm. "Well, off you go now!" she said, and then backed away from the truck.

George put the truck in reverse and started to drive out. He suddenly stopped the truck, and motioned to Rosalia to come to him. She walked back to the window, and he leaned out. His eyes met hers, and he reached for her hand. She allowed him to hold it. He pulled her in closer. "Rosa, dear," he said.

"Yes?" She stood there not knowing what he was going to say.

"Rosa ..." George looked up at the boys. They weren't letting anything get past their sight. George took another breath. "Rosa, ... I love you." He squeezed her hand and then moved his eyes from hers. She backed away from the truck once more, as he sped backwards out of the driveway. A smile crossed her face, which she had not had for a very long time.

He loves me? A small burst of joy filled her.

"Momma? Are you okay!?" Pablo hollered. They were unable to hear what they had been talking about.

Rosalia smiled again as she watched the truck disappear down the dirt road. She gritted her teeth, turned towards the boys, and said, "Yes." *I am more than okay*, she thought to herself.

Boss told Spud to follow behind him and not to say anything. The deal they were about to make could wind them both up in the prison for at least twenty years, and Boss wasn't about to be caught. He pulled out some yellow police tape and a couple of packsacks from his saddlebags and wandered over the bridge. He walked for about a quarter of a mile and strung the tape up across the road so that no one would come onto the bridge. He did the same at the other end. There wasn't much traffic in this area, so they weren't too concerned with police showing up. Once they attached the tape on both ends, they went down under the bridge to where the rest of the bikers were gathered. Boss slung one of the packs onto his back and Spud had the other. They walked through the crowd and refrained from making eye contact with any of them. If one stared too long, a brawl would break out. It was just the way it was when bikers who didn't know each other got together. Boss didn't like the feeling about this deal, but this was the only way he could get the amount of drugs he needed.

He continued through until he met up with the four men who were doing the dealing. They were underneath at the very back part of the bridge. The other bikers shielded them, in case someone who didn't belong there walked by. It would give them the appearance that it was just a bunch of bikers hanging around. Boss went up to the man who seemed to be responsible and told him how much he needed. The biker then went around the corner with another man. They returned with an armload of packages that were wrapped in brown paper and sealed with duct tape. Boss handed the biker the cash. He looked around as he counted it. Boss was nervous. Spud kept very close to him. He didn't dare say anything. The biker put out his hand, and Boss shook it. "Deal," he said. Boss took the drugs and stuffed them into his backpack and passed the rest to Spud. "Here, put these in your pack," Boss said. Spud didn't like the idea of having to transport these drugs, but Boss couldn't do it alone. They must have had over $1,000,000 worth of drugs under this bridge. If the police busted them, they would have a heyday. The bikers were mingling down there, but very closely; it was almost unbearable. Many bikers were making deals. The head biker motioned to Boss again. Boss went over to see what he wanted. He gave Boss some white stuff and ordered him to try it. Boss hesitated but did. Spud stayed silent.

chapter
17

Tunnel Bridge was just ahead, but Bernardo noticed that the area was blocked off by police tape. *What's going on here?* he thought. He pulled his truck alongside some bikes and got out.

There were approximately sixty bikes and a couple of trucks parked along the dirt road near the bridge. Bernardo heard some commotion from underneath the bridge, so he wandered down the pathway towards the noise. There in front of him were approximately seventy bikers. A few of them turned to look at him. Bernardo suddenly felt uneasy. *Why did I come down here? Why didn't I just drive off?* His curiosity usually got the best of him.

A few of the bikers surrounded Bernardo, so that he wouldn't be noticed by the rest under the bridge. One of them got really close. Bernardo noticed his name tag; it read Miguel. Then the rest circled him as if he were prey. Bernardo didn't say a word; although, there were whispers among some of the bikers.

Boss felt extremely high and had to sit down under the bridge by a few of the other bikers.

"Pretty good stuff, isn't it," another biker said to him.

Boss glanced over at him. The other man was almost to the point where he didn't know what was going on.

"Sure," Boss said. He usually didn't try the drugs he bought, but he wasn't going to argue with the rest of them. Spud had taken the packsack from Boss so it would be less weight for him to carry. They would need to leave as soon as possible, and they couldn't keep the yellow tape up much longer or people would start to wander down there to see what was going on. Boss stood up again and leaned on Spud. He glanced over to his right. He could have sworn that he had seen Whiskey's brother heading off with some of the others. Boss then thought it was the drugs making him hallucinate.

"What's your name?" Miguel asked Bernardo.

Bernardo wasn't sure how to answer this man. All the other bikers had totally surrounded him.

"What are you doing down here? Were you invited?" Another biker forced his way through to Bernardo.

"I said, what's your name?" Miguel was getting angry now.

Bernardo stepped backwards, but he wasn't going very far.

"Look, I took a wrong turn is all," he said.

"Hahaha, he took a wrong turn," Miguel mimicked. He grabbed Bernardo's throat and squeezed slightly, lifting Bernardo off his heels and onto his toes. He gagged. Two other bikers had grabbed his arms so that he couldn't swing at Miguel. Bernardo was confused.

"You realize, that we cannot let you go, since you know what is going on down here, right?" said one of the bikers.

Miguel let go of Bernardo's throat. Bernardo fell to his knees.

"What do you think we should do with him?" Miguel asked, looking around at the others.

One of the bikers in the background said, "Just let him go!"

"What? Are you fucking crazy?" Miguel said. Meanwhile, Bernardo stayed low, while trying to figure a way out of there. Miguel bent down and grabbed Bernardo's wallet; it was sticking partially out of his back pocket. Bernardo attempted to grab it, but he missed.

Miguel opened it up and looked at his ID. "Bernardo Gomez, is it?" He threw the wallet and ID at Bernardo. "So, how is your little brother doing? He's lucky he wasn't killed with the shit he's been doing," Miguel said.

Bernardo looked up at Miguel. "How do you know my brother?"

"I happened to be in the area, when he needed a lift to the hospital," Miguel said. "When I should have just ended his misery then and there."

"Then why didn't you? Why did you help him?" Bernardo was very confused.

"I'm not ready for murder charges ... yet," he responded. "But seeing as you seem to know more than he does, we can't take the chance of it leaking out, can we?" Miguel grabbed the hair on the top of Bernardo's head and pulled it backwards, so that Bernardo was now looking up at him.

"Well, what do you boys say? Shall we?" Miguel asked.

"I told you, I took a wrong turn, that was it," Bernardo pleaded. He was extremely worried that his life was in jeopardy. He did notice that these bikers had different patches on their vests than the others. There must have been more than one group under the bridge. *George must be involved with these bikers,* Bernardo thought. *Damn him. Thank God I got him off the farm when I did, or Rosalia and the boys would be in danger.*

The bikers huddled closer as they brought Bernardo to his feet. The other club had already left from under the bridge, so they didn't have to worry about anyone seeing them. They dragged Bernardo up the trail to the road. While he tried to fight them off, one of the bikers thumped him in the back of the head with the butt of his pistol and knocked him out. They put him in the back of Miguel's truck. Miguel dug in Bernardo's pockets until he found his truck keys. He passed them to one of the other bikers, who was riding two-up, so he could drive Bernardo's truck behind them.

"Okay, looks like the rest are leaving now. It should be safe," Spud said. Spud wasn't so sure Boss would be able to ride his bike in his condition. They stumbled up the bank and towards the road. There were only a few bikes left, and a pickup truck. Some of the other bikers had already removed the tape. Spud steadied Boss while he straddled his bike. "Are you sure you can ride?"

"Sure, I'm fine," Boss said.

Spud decided to put most of the drugs into the saddlebags on his bike, just in case Boss crashed, then it wouldn't be strewn all over the highway. Spud would talk with Boss when they got back to the clubhouse. He wasn't going to tolerate taking a chance like this again. If anything had gone wrong with this deal they all would've been taken down.

Boss wasn't too steady on his bike and Spud was worried about him. He flagged him down and suggested that they pull off the road until the high wore off. Boss didn't want to, but felt it was most likely for the best that they did. They pulled off the road and sat down in the bushes for a while. Spud sat impatiently, hoping it would wear off soon, but it would depend on how potent the drug was. It could last for hours. He looked over at Boss who was now facedown in the bushes. He had passed out.

Just great. "Damn, we're going to be here all fucking night!" Spud said angrily.

Spud and Boss were back on their bikes early the next morning. Boss apologized to Spud, which shocked him, because he usually didn't apologize to anyone. They headed down the road towards the clubhouse. Once there, they removed their packs from the bikes and detached their saddlebags. They took them inside. This room was where they kept the drugs. They placed the bags on the table and locked the doors behind them as they headed back upstairs.

"Sure was a different deal this time, wasn't it Boss?"

"Yeah, very different. I don't like dealing that way and will try to avoid it in the future. There were just way too many people around for my liking," Boss said. "For all we know some could have been narcs." He pulled out a cold beer from the cooler. "Want one, Spud?"

"Yes, I could use one." The men sat down at the table.

"I could have sworn I saw Whiskey's brother yesterday, down under the bridge," Boss said.

"Really?" Spud said. "Are you sure?"

"Well ... not really; I was high you know. But damn, something keeps nagging at me that it was him."

Spud got up. The first beer went down too quickly. "Want another?"

Boss nodded and reached his hand out. "We better watch our backs ..." Boss took a swig of his beer and let out an enormous belch.

Rosalia hadn't heard from George in a few days and was starting to worry. She hoped he was okay and had found a place to stay. Before he'd left, she wanted to run back out to him and tell him about Bernardo's note, but felt it wasn't the right thing to do at the time. Now, she thought otherwise. She figured if George called or came over for a visit, then she would tell him.

The boys were out in the barn getting their bikes. Rosalia figured they might as well ride them as much as they could before their dad came home. Who knows what Bernardo would do with the bikes when he returned. She went inside to see if she could occupy herself with something else to take her mind off things.

Marcus got off his bike and neglected to push the kickstand down. The bike started to fall over, and he quickly jumped out of the way before it fell on top of him. He looked over at Pablo. Marcus was embarrassed.

"What are you doing?" Pablo said patiently.

"I ... I." Marcus was sitting on the ground watching the front tire of his bike spin until it slowed to a stop. He was feeling sick to his stomach. There was a noise behind him. He looked over his shoulder and saw the front door open. Rosalia was standing there with her hands on her hips. Pablo could tell she was very upset. He put his kickstand down and got off his bike. "I'm going to see Momma. She doesn't look well." Pablo ran up the front steps and put his arms around his mother. She held him tightly. "It's okay, Momma. We're here."

"Pablo, I can't handle this anymore."

"I know, Momma. Let's sit down." Pablo and Rosalia sat down on the front steps. Marcus watched them. He wished he were close to his mother as Pablo was, but there was no point in competing. He struggled with his bike trying to get it back up. It was no use. He wasn't strong enough. Pablo would have to help him. Marcus spotted some gas leaking from the tank, soaking the dirt beneath the bike. "Pablo!" Marcus turned and waved at him.

"Be right back, Momma. I think Marcus needs help." Pablo ran out to where Marcus was. "What is it now?"

"I can't get my bike up, and it's leaking gas all over the friggin' place!"

"Okay, don't panic," Pablo said. "I remember watching Uncle George pick his bike up before." Pablo turned his back towards the bike, squatted and placed his lower back against the seat. Grabbing onto the frame with his hands he then pushed upwards with his legs and butt, and slowly lifted the bike.

"Wow, Pablo! That was cool!" Marcus was excited now. "Can I give it a try?"

"Sure, just a minute while I set it back down." Pablo eased the bike to the ground and got out of the way. "Now do what I just did." Pablo couldn't wait to see Marcus try. He silently giggled to himself.

Rosalia watched from the porch. She was proud of Pablo. He was always so patient with Marcus.

Marcus lowered himself and positioned his back and legs against the bike like Pablo had done. "Grab here." Pablo showed him where the best spots to hold were. Marcus listened and did as Pablo instructed. "Now, using your legs and butt, walk it up." Marcus let out some grunts and groans until he finally lifted the bike. Just as he got it to an upright position, he pushed a little too hard. "Oh, shit!" Marcus yelled. The bike toppled over onto the other side. Marcus lost his balance and fell on top of it. It took a moment until he realized what just happened, and both Pablo and he started laughing. Rosalia was now at the bottom of the stairs. She was laughing so hard that tears were streaming from her eyes.

"I think I'm too strong," Marcus said boisterously.

"No, Marcus. It's not that. You didn't put the kickstand down once you had it upright." Pablo chuckled, bursting Marcus' enthusiasm.

"Well, you didn't tell me to do that! Marcus got up and started chasing Pablo around the yard. Pablo couldn't stop laughing. He rounded a corner, tripped on a rock and then fell onto the dirt. Marcus jumped on top of him and started wrestling with him. Pablo knew he was just horsing around, so they wrestled for a few minutes until they heard their mother tell them it was enough. That was one thing they could never do, and that was stop before someone got hurt, unless someone told them to. The boys got up and brushed themselves off. Rosalia walked over to them.

"Okay, Marcus. Now go and try it again," Pablo said, while he brushed the dirt off of his jeans.

Marcus tried it again, and this time Pablo made sure he had the kickstand down first. Once Marcus up-righted the bike, Pablo helped him settle it onto the kickstand.

"Thanks, Pablo," Marcus said. "I actually think I learnt something today!"

"Okay boys, I think we should put the bikes away," Rosalia said. "We need to get some work done around here." She got up and headed out to the backyard to put some laundry on the line. While she was doing this, the boys rode their bikes to the barn.

Rosalia was heartbroken when George had left. Thankfully, she had hope, since he had told her he loved her. She appreciated that she wasn't the only one feeling it. There was a thread of guilt; she knew it was wrong for her to feel this way because she was married to his brother. But she could not get George out of her mind. She couldn't remember when she first started having these feelings for him, but it had been quite a while. How was she going to face Bernardo now that she knew how George felt about her? She was torn. Rosalia continued hanging up the laundry, whistling cheerfully under her breath.

George drove the truck into the driveway. He hadn't seen the boys or Rosalia for a few days; it had felt like forever. He knocked on the front door, but there was no answer. He waited a few minutes and tried again; still no answer. He quietly walked in. "Rosa?"

George wandered through the sitting room and then into the kitchen. The back door was ajar. He peeked out. Rosalia was sitting on the back step looking out towards the barn. The sound of the screen door opening startled her. "George!" She quickly stood up and almost fell down the steps. George caught her. "Hope I didn't scare you."

Rosalia smiled her sweet smile. "No. Not at all." She lied, but what did it matter. "How *are* you?"

"Good. Well, considering ..."

"It's great to see you! The boys will be very happy. They're out in the barn putting their bikes away."

"Oh? So they finally got them out, did they?" George commented.

"Yes," Rosalia said. "I figure they'd better get some riding in before they lose the bikes."

"Well, let's hope that doesn't happen," George said. "If I have my way, they won't need to worry."

I'm glad you showed them how to ride before you left, because I sure wouldn't have been able to. Would you like some coffee?" Rosalia asked as she turned to go inside.

"Sure. Here, let me get the door for you," George said.

He watched as she entered the house. The light summer dress she was wearing was made of cotton; it was worn and thin enough to see the silhouette of her body through. He had missed her. Once they were in the house, Rosalia remembered what he had said to her when he had left. She turned to look at him. As soon as she did, she was in his arms, and he kissed her deeply.

"I meant what I said," he told her, as if he was reading her mind. "I love you."

Rosalia kissed him back and repeated the words to him. "I love you too, George." She didn't think she would ever say that to anyone, except Bernardo.

"Now, where's that coffee?" George said, trying to change the subject. He knew if he didn't he would be sidetracked for the day and then nothing would get accomplished.

They sat at the kitchen table enjoying their coffee, when Rosalia said, "George, I need to show you something. I should have shown you before you left, but I didn't feel it was the best time."

"Sure, Rosa," he said. He pushed his chair back a bit and got comfortable.

Rosalia got up and went to her bedroom. She returned shortly with the crumpled piece of paper that Bernardo had left for her.

"Here, read this." She passed the paper to George, and sat back down across from him.

George opened it carefully, so as not to rip it. He read the note.

"What do you think he means?" asked Rosalia.

George put the paper down. He thought for a moment. "Rosa, dear ..." He didn't want to alarm her, but he knew his brother well. "I don't think Bernardo is coming back."

Rosalia held back her tears; she was upset, but she had already set in her mind that Bernardo wasn't returning. She just needed some clarification from someone else. "I see." Rosalia seemed a bit lost for a few minutes, and then she finally said, "George, ... will you come back home?"

George looked at her. "Are you sure, Rosa? What about Bernardo?"

"Yes, I have never been this sure about anything in my life, George. I will deal with Bernardo ... if and when he comes back."

There was no hesitation in George's voice. "I will, Rosa. I will come home for you and the boys." He reached over to her hand and held it. "Hey, how about we surprise them?"

"That would be great!" said Rosalia excitedly. "How should we do it?"

"I'll take off now, get my things packed, and then I'll return tomorrow," George said. He rose to his feet. "But don't tell them anything."

"They will be so excited, George!" Rosalia happily grabbed him and kissed him.

George wasn't able to hold back any longer. He held her tight and caressed her soft skin. His hands slid down the cotton fabric of her dress. He desired her, but knew he had to wait. They kissed for a few moments. He wound his fingers through her thick dark hair. "I'm sorry Rosa, ... soon. I must go before the boys see me."

He patted her behind, and reluctantly left through the front door. Rosalia ran out to the porch and watched his truck leave.

Damn him, she said to herself. She went into the farmhouse and headed into the kitchen. The boys would be hungry by now. She busied herself preparing their lunch and always made sure they were fed well. As she was cooking she was singing to herself; she was in an extremely good mood.

Fifteen minutes later, the boys came running through the back door. Rosalia turned and smiled at them.

"Hungry?" she said happily.

The boys looked at each other. They had noticed a change in their momma's mood, not that they didn't mind, it was just so surprising to them.

Rosalia developed a migraine that night and wasn't able to sleep any longer; things had finally caught up to her. She got up and went into the kitchen to make herself some tea. The house was extremely quiet. She poured the hot water into her cup and let her tea steep for a few minutes.

Rosalia had discussed with the boys a few days ago that their dad may not be coming back. She couldn't tell them much more, because she didn't know what was going on. The boys were upset, but not nearly upset as she had anticipated. They had been without their dad so much over the last few years that they would get over it soon enough. She never told them that George was moving back home, although she found it difficult not to tell them. She didn't know how to tell the boys about George and her. She felt it was too soon.

Marcus and Pablo took turns looking through the book in their room. "So, Uncle George belongs to this club?" Marcus said.

"Yes, well he did, but apparently he's not involved anymore," Pablo said reassuringly.

"Did you ask him about Dad?" Marcus asked curiously.

"What do you mean?"

"About where he goes?" Marcus said.

"We still don't know. Dad said it was for work. Maybe Uncle George will tell us soon."

"Pablo, what are we going to do now that Dad is gone?" Marcus said. "Momma said he won't be coming back. Do you think he's in trouble?" Marcus tried to remain calm the best he could, but then started to cry. One minute he seemed to care about his dad and another he despised him; it was like a love/hate relationship.

"Well, we have to go on without him, Marcus. I know it's tough, but we can't just shut down. Momma needs us."

"It's going to be so hard without him ...," Marcus started to say. He had it set in his mind that he would never see his dad again.

"Marcus, I know ... hey, maybe we should go do something to take our minds off things for a bit?" Pablo suggested.

"Sure ..." Marcus looked up at him gloomily. He didn't seem to be in the mood to do much of anything.

"Let's go for a ride!" Pablo said excitedly.

"Nah, I don't feel like going around in circles right now," Marcus said.

"No, Marcus. Let's take the bikes to town," Pablo said.

"What? Are you crazy? You know Momma will be upset if she finds out!" Marcus hollered.

"Sure, she might. But she's resting and won't even notice," Pablo said sneakily.

"Well ... okay," Marcus said. He felt adrenaline rushing through him.

The boys ran out to the barn and pushed their bikes out. Pablo closed the barn doors. They fired up their bikes and let them idle briefly. Luckily, they weren't too close to the farmhouse. Once the bikes were warm, the boys put their helmets on. Pablo instructed Marcus to take the long way around the house. They hoped their momma wouldn't notice that they were gone.

Marcus followed Pablo as they rode the bikes around the outside perimeter of the house. Now that Marcus had had more practice, he was feeling more at ease on his bike. The boys headed to the end of their property, and Pablo pointed as to which way they were going. They looked back towards the farm; it didn't appear that their momma noticed or she would have been out on the front porch hollering at them. They pulled out onto the dirt road and headed in the direction of town.

Neither of them had license plates on their bikes nor did they have insurance. At this point, Pablo didn't care. He was hurting regarding his dad, and the only way he could think of putting it on the back burner was to go for a ride.

The boys rode side-by-side down the road, as they had seen many bikers do. They loved the feeling of the wind in their face. It was a feeling you couldn't explain. They now understood why their uncle loved riding as much as he did.

The bikes each had half a tank of gas, so they should make it to town and back with no problem. They would have to be careful if they were to see any state police, because if they were pulled over they may lose their bikes. Pablo pointed at a side road for them to take so it would take them off the main road. Pablo had driven this road many times before in the truck. He knew the way to town using various routes, which was good. Marcus, on the other hand, never really paid attention to directions because he was always the passenger and it didn't matter to him how they got there, as long as they did. Marcus looked at his brother off and on as they continued riding. The smile on Marcus' face was priceless. Pablo felt like he didn't have a worry in the world.

After ten minutes on the road, they made another turn that would take them into town. Pablo pulled over to the side of the road before they went into town and Marcus followed him. They turned the bikes off.

"Okay, we're going to pull into another road up there," Pablo said as he pointed to his right. "We'll park the bikes there so that no one sees them, and then we can walk the rest of the way, okay?"

"Sure," Marcus said. For the most part, he was agreeable with Pablo's decisions.

They got back on their bikes and rode up the road a bit before Pablo signalled to the right, and they turned off the road. They went up a little hill and parked the bikes near some bushes.

"This looks good," Pablo said. Marcus nodded. They ran down

the hill and then walked towards town. About a quarter of a mile down the road, Pablo spotted something bright and shiny in the ditch. "Hey, Marcus, let's check that out!" he hollered with excitement.

The boys ran over to the ditch and slid down. The reflecting metal was sticking out of a bunch of twigs and branches. Marcus and Pablo started pulling the debris off. Pablo stopped suddenly. "Marcus, do you see what I see?"

Marcus looked. It didn't alert him right away, until after Pablo pointed out that what they just found was a motorcycle. "Come on. Let's get this shit off of it!" Pablo said.

The boys frantically tore a bunch of the debris from off and around the bike.

Pablo reached underneath, behind the kickstand and yanked on something, but it wasn't coming off. He reached into his pocket and pulled out his jackknife.

"What are you doing, Pab?" Marcus asked.

"Just a minute," he said. He reached under the bike with both hands and cut the strap that was holding the object to the bike. He gave the object a quick yank and then held it tightly in his hand. With his free hand he pressed the back of the blade of the knife on his leg, so he could close it. He then stuffed the knife back into his pocket.

"Marcus, I think it's Uncle George's bike!" Pablo said.

"How do you know it's his?" Marcus said. "I mean, there are probably hundreds of people around that have the same bike."

Marcus looked. Pablo opened his hand, inside was a small, silver bell. "Now do you see?" Marcus nodded.

"This is the bell that Dad bought for Uncle George for Christmas a few years ago," Pablo said. He shoved the bell into the front pocket of his jeans.

"Why do you think his bike is here? I mean, if he was in an accident, wouldn't they have had it in the impound yard?" Marcus said.

"Yes, they would have. We're going to have to talk to Uncle George about this when he comes back. Let's get it covered up again before someone sees us," Pablo said.

The boys looked both ways and quickly covered the bike back up. "I think we should go straight home," Pablo said. Marcus agreed. The boys turned around and ran back down the road and up the hill to where they had stashed their bikes.

chapter

18

WHILE THE BOYS WERE IN TOWN, George had returned to the farm with his belongings, hoping to surprise them. As soon as he entered the house, Rosalia was in his arms. He dropped his bags and put his arms around her. They kissed for a moment. George took Rosalia's hand and led her to his former bedroom. Rosalia turned and looked into his eyes. He had moved his hands up to her face and gently held her. The anticipation of his kiss was driving her crazy. There were no words spoken. He kissed her lips softly at first and then again. He lowered his hands down the sides of her light cotton dress. He could almost feel her skin beneath. His touch was soft. Rosalia had put her arms around him and pulled him in closer. She could feel his desire as he pressed his body against hers. As they kissed more passionately, George traced the form of her body; he knew her skin would feel like velvet. He slowly pulled her dress upwards until he felt the softness of her hips. He rested his hands on either side and pulled her even closer. Rosalia felt his hands tighten. She knew he wouldn't be able to hold back any longer and neither would she. Rosalia let go of him and lifted her dress up and slipped it off. She dropped it to the floor. George kissed her longer this time. His body was yearning for hers. He reached behind him and closed the bedroom door.

George moved towards the bed and they lay down. They kissed and caressed each other until neither of them could stop. Finally, they made love, not once but twice. Rosalia lay spent in his arms. She had totally forgotten what she had wanted to talk to him about earlier. She closed her eyes and fell asleep. George got up after a while, had a shower, and then got dressed. He went out the back porch to have a cigarette. Life was good.

Rosalia surprised him shortly after. She hadn't slept that long. She was full of smiles and giggles. She bent over and kissed him on the forehead. "I love you, George," she said.

"I love you too, Rosa," he said.

Once she finished cleaning up, she returned to the back porch. She sat beside George.

"So, where are the boys?" George asked curiously.

Rosalia turned her head. She was ashamed at what the boys had done and wasn't sure how to break the news to him. Finally, she just blurted it out. "The boys took the bikes off the property. I don't know where they are," she said. She was extremely worried about them.

George sat beside Rosalia. He wasn't sure how to respond. It was his fault; he should have never helped them buy the bikes. He hoped they were okay. "Look, Rosa, we'll talk to them when they get back. There's no sense in getting too worried unless there's something to be concerned about. I am sure they are just fine," George said. He took her hand in his. She turned to look at him, and he lifted her chin and kissed her lips tenderly. Rosalia smiled.

"I hope you're right," she said. "I'm glad you're home, George. I missed you."

"I missed you more than you know," George said.

"So, George, where did you stay?" Rosalia asked, making conversation.

He stood up over by the railing and lit a cigarette. He didn't like smoking beside Rosalia. "I rented a room at a motel. They rent out by the month now. It wasn't very big, but it was okay for what I needed," he said. "I hadn't unpacked very much, so it was easy to just pack up and leave."

Rosalia looked up and saw some dust rising out on the dirt road. She watched intently, and then she rushed out to the front porch. George remained on the back porch, while he finished his cigarette.

Rosalia didn't understand how the boys could do this, especially after she and their uncle had told them many times it was against the rules. She paced back and forth on the wooden slats. *Why, why, why.*

The boys headed towards the farmhouse. They pulled the bikes into the yard and quickly parked them. They ran up the front steps and almost into their momma. She stopped them in their tracks. "What the hell do you think you're doing?!"

Pablo felt bad, but he hoped she would understand after he told her what they found. "Momma, please, you have to listen."

Rosalia was very upset with them and she kept hollering.

George walked out to the front porch and tried to calm her.

The boys were in shock, because they had no idea their uncle was there.

Rosalia huffed and sat down on one of the chairs.

"Why, Pablo?" George asked with disappointment in his eyes.

"Listen, Uncle George," Pablo said. "Can we talk?"

"Sure, how about we all sit down and talk this out," George calmly suggested.

They all sat down. Pablo wasn't sure how to start, so he said, "George, how were you hurt?"

George looked at Pablo. "Now what does that have to do with you boys taking off?"

"Trust me." When Pablo said this to George, George knew he was serious.

"Okay son." He sighed deeply. "I'm not sure," he finally said.

"Was it a motorcycle accident?" Pablo asked. "Because you never did bring your bike home."

Hmmm, George thought for a moment. "No, it wasn't. Honestly, I don't know what happened, and I don't know where my bike is."

Rosalia was nervously shaking and tapping her feet.

Marcus was too anxious to hold back the news. He rose to his feet and said excitedly, "We found your bike!"

"What?" George said shocked.

"We found your bike!" Marcus repeated. Rosalia calmed herself and listened carefully.

"Where?" George was now very interested in what the boys had to say.

"In a ditch, just before town," Pablo said.

"Really? Are you sure it's mine?"

"Yes, Uncle George," Pablo reached into his pocket and pulled the tarnished bell out and handed it to George.

George stared at the bell. It was indeed the bell from his bike.

Rosalia got to her feet quickly and took the bell from George. Tears filled her eyes. "George ... it is ... it is the bell that Bernardo bought you. I was with him. She turned the bell over and rubbed the debris and oil off the best she could with the corner of her apron. Inscribed on the back of the bell was his name, and an angel etched on the front of it. George put his arm around her and gently squeezed. "My God, where did you find it Pablo? Can you show me?"

"Yes. Let's go! I'll take you right to it!"

Rosalia knew there was no use in punishing the boys this time. After all, something good had come out of it.

George went out to the truck with his nephews. "We'll be back in a bit, Rosa!" He waved to her. Rosalia waved and clutched the bell tightly in her hand.

Pablo drove the truck to where they had found the bike. George got out of the truck and watched as the boys unburied the bike.

"Holy shit! My bike!" George said. He slid down the embankment into the ditch where the boys were.

"It doesn't look like there's too much damage either, Uncle George," Pablo said.

"Good! Now all we have to do is get it home," George said.

"Home?" Pablo said curiously. "Where is home?"

George hesitated, and then said, "The farm, Pab." He smiled at both the boys; they understood—George had moved back home. Marcus had the biggest grin he could muster.

"We could call a tow company and have them bring it home?"

Pablo suggested.

"Yes, but we shouldn't leave the bike alone, especially now that it's visible," George said.

"I can stay with it," Pablo said.

"Good idea. You stay with the bike, and I'll go and call the tow truck," said George. "I'll drive to town and call from a phone booth. Then we'll meet you back here. Once the tow truck gets the bike loaded, we can head home."

"Okay, get going then," Pablo said excitedly.

George and Marcus climbed back into the truck.

Pablo sat on the side of the road near the ditch. He waited patiently. He was still remembering how those bikers had known about George's release from the hospital. He felt that they could appear at any moment. Finally, a tow truck came around the corner. Pablo stood up. He hoped his uncle would be back shortly. Pablo didn't want to have to lie about why the bike was in the ditch, but knew if he pretended it was his bike then his uncle wouldn't have to worry about involving the law. If his uncle had been in an accident, then he would have to answer questions he had no answers to. The tow truck pulled up to the side of the road and the driver jumped out. "What do we have here, son?" The driver looked down into the ditch.

"I went off the road," Pablo lied.

"I see that. That's a mighty big bike for a lad your size."

"Are you able to get it out?" Pablo asked.

"Sure, that's my job," the driver said cheerfully.

Pablo looked down the road and saw his uncle's truck. *Phew*, he thought.

His uncle drove up ahead of the tow truck, climbed out of the truck and walked over to Pablo. "Hey son, I'm glad to see you're not hurt."

"No, I'm good ... Dad." Pablo grinned.

"Good. When we get it home we'll have a look at the damage."

After the tow truck driver and George got the bike out of the ditch, they pushed it up the ramp and onto the flatbed. The driver tied it down so it would be secure and not fall over.

"What do we owe you?" George said.

The tow truck driver quoted him a price and George told him they would settle the cost once they got the bike home.

"Come on son, jump in the truck," George said to Pablo. The tow truck followed George as they headed back to the farm.

When they arrived home, the tow truck backed in as close to the barn as possible so that he could unload the bike inside. George and the boys had already opened the doors and moved stuff aside so the driver could back the bike down. Once the bike was off the flatbed, George paid the driver and sent him on his way.

The boys and George looked over the bike. "It will take a while to get this baby back on the road," George said. He looked at his watch. "Well, it's getting late. Let's go grab some dinner."

The boys locked the barn and walked with George back to the house. After they had all eaten, George decided it was time for the dreaded lecture to the boys about taking their bikes off the property. Rosalia had already put her plate in the sink and said goodnight.

George followed Rosalia into the sitting room. He said goodnight to her and kissed her cheek. "I'll talk to the boys," he said.

"Thank you, George." She went into her room and closed the door.

Marcus and Pablo overheard them in the other room. They were suspicious as to how they were acting. Before they could say anything, George walked into the kitchen. He sat down across from the boys.

"That wasn't a very smart thing to do today, Pablo," George said.

"I know, Uncle George. I guess I wasn't thinking. I know it was wrong."

"Well, at least you both made it back safely. Don't do it again. I don't think your Momma can handle much more stress."

"We understand," Pablo looked over at Marcus and nudged him.

"Okay," Marcus said.

"Clean up the kitchen when you're done, and then get some sleep." George got up and placed his dishes in the sink.

Before George left the room Pablo said, "George, we're glad you're home." George gave both the boys a hug and went off to his room.

While the boys were cleaning the kitchen, Pablo was lost in thought. He kept wondering how his uncle's bike had gotten into the ditch. *Is Uncle George in trouble? Is he hiding something? Why was he back? Why did he go?* Nothing made any sense.

George managed to get himself out to the barn quietly the next morning, so as not to disturb anyone. He had already started cleaning his bike and figuring out what he needed to do to make it road-worthy again. Pablo walked in shortly after, because he had noticed the barn door was open.

"Morning, Uncle George. You're up bright and early."

"Yes. Now, that I have something to do." He chuckled.

Pablo sat on a bench near the doorway and watched his uncle as he tediously washed his bike. "Sure takes a lot of work, doesn't it," Pablo said.

"Yes, it does, but I haven't cleaned it in ages it seems. It needs a good wash. Mind you, I should wait until it's fixed before I wash it, because it's just going to get dirty again." He laughed. "Oh well. Here, give me a hand!" He tossed Pablo a clean cloth. "Shine the chrome up."

Pablo jumped off the bench. He was always willing to help his uncle. Pablo figured now was a good time to ask his uncle some more questions. "Uncle George?"

"Yes."

"What's going on? I mean ... one minute you're here and the next minute you're gone?" Pablo asked.

George bent down on one knee so that he could clean the rim of the tire. "Your momma asked me to come back," he said.

"Oh? What about Dad? I thought he made you leave?" Pablo said concerned. He moved over to the other side of the bike and started shining the pipes.

George looked over at Pablo. "Yes, your dad had asked me to leave, Pablo, but your momma needs someone around the farm in case something happens." George hoped Pablo wouldn't go any further with the questions.

Pablo stood up and placed the cloth on the seat. He had so much going on inside of him and needed the answers. He wasn't going to give up easily.

"Uncle George, I heard you and Momma last night in the sitting room. What's going on?" Pablo said.

"Okay son, promise not to say anything to Marcus or your momma?"

Pablo stared at his uncle. "No, I won't promise. I'm tired of having to keep everything a damn secret around here!" He picked up the cloth and threw it at his uncle.

George stood up and walked over to Pablo. He put his arm around him. He knew Pablo was hurting.

"Fine," George said. There was a pause. "I will tell you the truth, and I don't expect you to be happy about it or keep it a secret."

Pablo looked up at his uncle. His uncle really did respect him.

"Okay," Pablo said. He waited.

George was quiet for a few minutes, while he gathered his thoughts. "Pablo, son, I have feelings for your momma, and she has feelings for me. I am not sure how to explain this to you."

Pablo had a feeling it was about that, so he wasn't overly surprised; as a matter of fact, he was pleased. He loved his dad, but he adored his uncle.

"Thank you for telling me, Uncle George," Pablo said. "I won't say anything to Momma or Marcus, unless they ask. I just didn't want anymore secrets."

George gave Pablo a hug. "I know, son."

Pablo decided to change the subject. "Can you tell me more about the oath you had to sign for 'Riders of Reason?'"

"Well son," George said. He walked over beside Pablo and they sat down on the bench. "I'm really not sure where to start. You see, a lot of the information I would like to tell you ... is forbidden."

"Forbidden? Why is that?" Pablo asked curiously.

"Well, you see ... when one signs an oath, it binds you to the club as 'family,' and no matter what, you have to fulfill what they want and need at all times. Don't get me wrong; there is nothing closer than a 'biker family.'

"Really? Then why?" Pablo shook his head. "Why, can't you tell me ... I'm family?"

George let out a chuckle. He didn't mean to, but his nephew had no idea what kind of 'family' the bike club was.

"What about the bikers who brought you home? Are they bad men? Are they going to come back?" Pablo asked concerned.

"No, Pablo. They won't be back. I won't be seeing them again," George said. He wasn't going to tell Pablo that he feared for his life and theirs. He was just happy that he was back on the farm so he could protect them.

"Are you sure? Is that why you're back home? Are we in danger?" Pablo stood up quickly.

George laughed. "No, Pablo. I think you're reading too much of that book. Maybe you should bring it to me and I'll get rid of it."

Pablo wasn't ready to give up the book, just yet. "Can I ask you one more question, and I promise I won't ask anymore?" Pablo felt how uncomfortable his uncle was talking about it.

"Sure, well, I hope I can answer it," George said.

"Does Dad belong to this club?" Pablo asked.

There was silence. *Damn kids,* George thought.

chapter

19

GEORGE HAD AGED HARD over the years. He was no longer working, and spent a lot of his time travelling. Rosalia was adamant she would never ride on his motorcycle. She preferred to stay home where it was safe. Since Bernardo's disappearance, she had pretty much isolated herself from everyone, except for George. The farm was the only life she knew.

He raised his hand to block the glaring evening sun. This was the worst time of the day to be riding. He pulled over to the side of the road to put his sunglasses on; the brightness was unbearable. Once he was back on the road, a GMC van sped past him. George wished he knew the road better, then it wouldn't have been so difficult.

The next corner bore to the right. Just as George started to guide the bike through the corner, he was blinded by another burst of light. He couldn't even make out the van in front of him now. He shielded the light with his right hand, which caused his bike to decelerate, making it cross the yellow line.

In the other lane, a 1974 Kenworth slammed on its brakes. You could smell the rubber of the tires as they melted into the pavement. The trailer buckled and swerved into the right lane, causing the cab of the semi to flip onto its side, pulling the trailer with it.

The impact was intense. George and the motorcycle hit the front of the semi head-on. George was thrown off his bike and landed on the embankment. There was no movement. The motorcycle took a solid hit and parts of it were littered across the road. The driver of the truck managed to climb out of the semi. He hobbled over to George, but it was too late. There was no pulse. The accident was fatal.

Pablo heard about the accident while he was watching the news. He was shocked and saddened. He immediately called Marcus. Marcus was heartbroken, and he knew his mother would be, too. Pablo wondered, if it was an accident, or if George was still involved with the motorcycle club, somehow. He hoped it had been just an accident. It was beginning to be too much for even Pablo to handle. He thought George had washed his hands of the club years ago.

George's memorial service was small. Rosalia had so wished her husband, Bernardo would have been able to attend it.

TIME PASSED. It had been a year now. Rosalia sat in the same spot she had sat in for the last few months—on the front porch, in the rickety chair that had seen long hot summers and frigid cold winters, watching down the dusty road. Every time she heard a truck, her head would rise slightly, with hope that it might be Bernardo. He had disappeared eleven years prior and everyone believed he was dead. There was no concrete evidence, so she continued to hold onto the hope in that he could still be alive.

Rosalia remembered that day well, when she received the call about Bernardo. She was never able to prove it though, and there was no body to bury. The call came in not long before George's accident. Rosalia thought it was a coincidence that she would hear then about her husband, and not sooner. The caller had said that Bernardo's body had been found and burned, with hardly anything left. There was nothing to bury; cremation, well, enough said. The caller said they had found his remains down in Ouro Preto, Brazil, which was over 2200 miles from San Rafael. Rosalia held a memorial service for her sons' sake. Still, something in the back of her mind kept telling her that he was alive, somewhere. Marcus and Pablo believed in their hearts that he was gone for good.

Bernardo had been her first love. But with him being away all the time, their bond diminished. She needed closure. Then George came into her life, and he was all she could think about—oh how she missed him.

Marcus and Pablo were now avid motorcyclists, and still resided on the farm with their momma. It was getting difficult for her to do much of anything anymore.

Marcus flicked on the lamp on the bedside table; it was 4:00 A.M. His stomach was doing back flips, anticipating the meeting with 'Riders of Reason.' Marcus stayed in his Uncle George's old room. He often imagined his uncle was still alive. Pablo was asleep up in the loft. He had no idea that Marcus was meeting with Davis, or that he had been involved with this club for some time. Davis was the 1st Officer of the motorcycle club, 'Riders of Reason.' Pablo and Marcus had separate interests now. Pablo was more of a home body and stayed close to his momma, while Marcus was reckless and wild; he hardly ever stayed home when he wasn't tending to the farm.

Marcus picked up a piece of paper that he had tossed on the table a few days prior. It was Davis' number. Marcus procrastinated, which he was always good at. He was instructed to call Davis at 5:00 A.M. Marcus threw the bed sheet off and got up out of bed. He would call Davis when he went outside, so that his momma and Pablo wouldn't overhear.

"Good morning son," Rosalia said, as he walked out of his room. "You're up early."

Marcus knew she would be awake; she had always been an early bird since he could remember. "Yeah, things to do, people to see."

"Pab going with you?"

"No, Momma."

"Coffee's on," she said.

Marcus walked over to his momma and kissed her on the forehead. He went into the kitchen and out the back door.

Davis sat at the table nursing his now cold coffee. His cell phone lay next to his cup. It was already after 5:00 A.M. He was tapping his fingers on the edge of the table, when suddenly his phone started to vibrate. He picked it up and answered, "Hello."

"Davis, it's Marcus."

"Great. I was wondering when you were going to call," Davis said. "I'm going to make this short. Meet me down in the alley where the old pizza joint used to be. Make sure you aren't followed. I'll be there in twenty." Davis hung up the phone before Marcus had a chance to respond.

Marcus put his phone into the front pocket of his jeans. He hated it when Davis was abrupt. He started up his bike. The rumbling could be heard a few blocks away due to the upgrade of the pipes a few months back. Marcus recalled his uncle saying many times, *"The louder the pipes, the less chance of a wipe" (meaning accident)*. Marcus always took his uncle's advice to heart, and whenever he was able to, he would follow it.

Marcus arrived in the alley thirty minutes later. He parked his bike alongside the pale brick wall of the former pizza parlour. The scent of stale pizza cartons still lingered in the closed-in area. Marcus glanced around. It was desolate here, and he imagined the only action was from the rats and the homeless people. The rat infestation was one of the reasons this part of town had ceased to exist. The lampposts were all tarnished and the bulbs had been missing for years. The graffiti all over the walls was fading from time. Marcus felt uncomfortable meeting here.

Marcus decided to stay with his bike until Davis showed up; even then, he wasn't certain he wanted to leave it there.

"Come on Davis, where are you?" Marcus whispered under his breath. He leaned against his bike and patiently watched the entrance to the alley. The scurrying of the rodents startled him from time to time. About twenty minutes later, Marcus could hear the familiar rumbling sounds as he saw silhouettes of some bikes coming towards the alley. There had to be at least ten bikes coming in, but none looked familiar. The bikers nodded to Marcus as they rode the bikes up ahead of his. They parked the bikes. One of the bikers dismounted and walked over to Marcus. He put out his hand and Marcus extended his. Out of respect, they shook hands.

"Davis here yet?" the biker asked.

"No, he should be shortly," Marcus said.

"Cool." The man walked back over to the other bikers.

Marcus noticed that they were wearing a club patch on the back of their jackets—it wasn't 'Riders of Reason.' Marcus recalled seeing the nametag on the man's jacket; it had read 'Torch.'

Marcus was always amazed at the nicknames that were chosen for bikers. They usually fit their personalities. This fellow named 'Torch' had fiery-red hair that hung just above his shoulders. He also sported a reddish-grey handlebar moustache and a full beard. When the fellow laughed his complexion turned bright red. Marcus imagined if anyone angered Torch, he would have quite the temper. *Torch was an excellent choice*, Marcus thought.

The bikers talked among themselves as if Marcus wasn't there.

Finally Davis' truck pulled into the alley. Marcus felt somewhat relieved that he was not alone. Davis got out of the truck, carrying a suitcase.

"Hey, Marcus!" Davis said, and gave him a brotherly hug.

"Hey, Davis!"

Davis took Marcus aside to talk to him.

"Who are these guys?" Marcus asked.

"I'll let you know later. Right now we have more to worry about."

"Oh?" Marcus wasn't sure what Davis was talking about.

"Look, let's take this inside." Davis turned to look at the other bikers. He motioned to the one who had said hi to Marcus that he would be a few minutes. The man nodded.

Davis and Marcus headed towards the empty building. Davis carefully slid open one of the broken windows and they crawled inside. There was debris and garbage all over and the odour was so intense that Marcus had to remove his bandana to cover his nose. He had no idea why they came to this part of town. Davis led him into another room. He set the suitcase on the floor, and then reached up to a grate. It appeared to be an entrance to a ventilation shaft. Davis pried the grate until it broke free. It was as if it had been there an extremely long time. Davis motioned to Marcus to help lift him up until he could pull himself inside the opening.

Davis crawled in about twenty feet, and then he returned, pulling another suitcase; it was identical to the one he had brought in from the truck. Marcus steadied Davis as he climbed back down. Davis pulled the suitcase out and then placed it gently on the floor; it had to weigh at least fifty pounds. Davis opened it. It was full of small packages, also known as bricks. While Marcus looked inside, Davis grabbed the empty suitcase and tossed it up into the shaft.

"What is this?" Marcus said.

Davis looked up at Marcus and laughed. "What, you don't know?" Davis reached in and took out one of the bricks. "See this," Davis said. "We have forty-eight of these babies. The cocaine is damn near pure, too. We're talking thousands of dollars worth, close to a million to be exact." Davis placed the brick back into the suitcase and pulled out a smaller package that had been tucked in the top compartment. "Now, this here," he said, "is a G-Pack." He opened it up, and Marcus looked inside.

"Usually, there are one hundred of these in a G-Pack, but there are only twenty-five left in this one." Davis looked as though he knew where the rest had gone, and he hadn't mentioned selling them.

"Ahhh!" Marcus said. "I didn't realize ..." He stopped talking. He wasn't sure what to say, and didn't want Davis to think he didn't know anything about cocaine.

"It's been in here for a few days. I needed to check it out before calling the others inside." Davis quickly put the small package into his jacket pocket and closed the suitcase. "There's another full suitcase up there," he said, "but we won't tell them it's here." He tapped the grate back into place, so that the other bikers wouldn't suspect anything.

"You wait here. Guard this with your life," Davis said. "I'll be right back."

Marcus was uneasy being left alone with the drugs. He waited patiently. *This was a huge deal*, he thought. All of a sudden, he felt extremely nervous. *Hurry up, Davis!* he thought, and he started pacing the room.

Pablo had been concerned about Marcus for a while. He never told Marcus that he had suspected that he was involved in a motorcycle club. Pablo didn't want to alarm his momma as she had her own share of ups and downs over the years. Pablo needed to find out what was going on with Marcus, but he needed to do it without him knowing. Pablo figured as long as Marcus wasn't doing anything illegal, he wouldn't say anything to his momma. He just needed to know for himself that everything was genuine. Pablo didn't like or approve of sneaking around behind people's backs, but he felt he had good reasons. He would wait until his momma went to town before he searched Marcus' room to see if he could find anything.

The doors had all been boarded up from the outside, so Davis went back through the same window, in which they had entered earlier. He carefully climbed out and headed over to the others. He walked up to Torch. "Okay, let's do this." He had known Torch from a previous engagement.

The two of them went inside the building. The rest of the bikers outside were instructed to keep an eye open for anyone. Davis and Torch entered the room where Marcus was. Marcus had stepped back, closer to the entrance of the room. There were some words spoken between Davis and Torch, but Marcus was too far away to hear. Davis turned the suitcase towards Torch.

"You sure it's all there?" Torch asked.

"Yes. I mean, there is another suitcase but I only brought one," Davis said. "You act as if you don't trust me."

Torch didn't comment. "Open it up," he said. "Trust is to be earned, not taken for granted."

Davis opened the suitcase.

While Torch was looking, Davis pulled out the package from his pocket.

Torch looked up quickly, and then backed away. "No sudden moves, man," he said.

"I was just getting some stuff for you to test," Davis said. He opened the bag and pulled out a small clear vial and handed it to Torch.

Torch opened the vial and put some of the white powder on his index finger. He then ran his finger along his gums. The powder had a bitter taste to it. They waited for a few minutes until Torch said, "Yup, that's good," as he felt his gums go numb.

Davis closed the suitcase. "Deal?"

"How much is in this suitcase?" Torch asked.

"Twenty-four kilos, and another twenty-four in the other suitcase," Davis said.

"That's quite a haul," Torch said. He stood there for a moment, thinking. "It's a bit more than we had discussed, but it shouldn't be a problem. Meet me back here at midnight with both, and then we'll finish the deal."

Davis reached out his hand to Torch. "Deal." The men shook hands. Torch turned around, nodded to Marcus and left the building. Davis waited until he had heard the bikes start up, and then he tossed the package with the vials back into the suitcase. He removed the grate and pulled the empty suitcase out. He placed it on the floor. After the full one was placed back in the shaft, Marcus helped him climb up to push the suitcase further in. Davis came back out and then secured the grate. "Now, when we come back we won't need to bring anything."

Davis grabbed the empty suitcase, and he and Marcus went out through the window. Davis looked over his shoulder to make sure there was no one around. It looked clear. He disliked having to leave all the drugs there, but he didn't have a choice. He needed them out of his hands.

"Marcus, you must keep this quiet. See you at midnight," Davis said. He patted him on the back and headed for his truck. Marcus looked over his shoulder as well. He didn't like this feeling of fear.

Just after Rosalia pulled out of the driveway, Pablo went into Marcus' room. He started with the dresser drawers. *Such an obvious place to hide things.* He spent a good twenty minutes going through the room. Just before he gave up, he spotted the corner of a book sticking out from under a pile of clothes on the floor of the closet. Marcus had never been known for being tidy. Pablo pulled the book out and held it in his hands. He sat on the edge of the bed and thumbed through the pages. It had been a few years since he'd even thought about looking in it. He wondered how long Marcus had had it, and if maybe this was the club Marcus was hanging out with. Pablo prayed it wasn't.

chapter

20

MARCUS RETURNED to the farm an hour later. It was still early. He noticed a light on in his room and could have sworn he had shut it off when he left. He shook his head. He may have forgotten. His momma's car was not in the driveway, so he pulled his bike in.

Pablo heard Marcus' bike come in, and he quickly left his room, with the book in hand. He was going to confront Marcus once and for all as to what was going on. He hoped that Marcus would tell him.

Pablo opened the front door just as Marcus was nearing the top of the steps. "Hey, Man!"

Marcus gave his usual nod and walked past Pablo and into the farmhouse. "Momma out?"

"Yes. She had to run some errands."

Marcus noticed the book in Pablo's hand.

Pablo raised it up. "How long have you had this?"

Marcus kicked his boots off and walked towards the kitchen. "Oh ... a while now."

Pablo followed Marcus. "What do you mean a while?"

"It's not like it's a big secret, Pab."

Pablo slammed the book down on the kitchen table. He knew he should have gotten rid of it a long time ago. But because it was their uncle's, he felt obligated to keep it.

Marcus turned around and glared at Pablo.

"Why do you have it?" Pab questioned. "Why?"

"Pab, settle down."

"I ain't gonna settle down! I want to know ..."

Marcus knew what Pablo was going to say, but he refused to willingly offer the answers Pablo wanted to hear.

Pablo grabbed Marcus' arm and forcefully pushed him against the wooden storage unit. The contents of the cupboard rattled from the sudden impact. Marcus struggled with his brother, but from years of experience, and Pablo's much larger size, Marcus could put up a good fight but always ended up on the bottom.

Pablo's firm grip held Marcus in such a way that he wasn't able to free himself. Marcus was getting frustrated. "Fuck, Man!" Marcus yelled.

"Are you going to tell me now ... how long you've been involved with them?"

Just before Marcus said anything, they heard their momma struggling with the door knob on the back door.

"I'll talk with you later!" Pablo said and released his hold on Marcus.

Marcus adjusted his clothing, grabbed the book, went into his room and closed the door. He couldn't believe his brother had gone through his room behind his back.

Pablo opened the back door and helped his momma with the grocery bags. Together they put away the food. He was furious with Marcus.

Rosalia sensed something was very wrong at the dinner table that night. She knew her sons well, and this wasn't like them not to have conversations while eating.

"Everything okay, guys?"

Marcus wasn't all that hungry, so he excused himself from the table. He put his plate on the corner of the counter and went out to the back porch. He lit up a cigarette. It was only minutes before Pablo joined him. They sat side-by-side on the back steps, looking out towards the barn. Many evenings they sat there, just staring off into the night.

"Well ..." Pab said. His tone had settled now.

"Like I said, it's been a while, Pab," Marcus took a long drag from his cigarette.

"Why didn't you tell me?"

"I guess ... because, I knew you had been doing your best to keep it from me all these years, and I didn't want to upset you. I knew you wouldn't approve."

"Well, I don't, and never will!"

"Didn't think so."

"So how deeply *are* you involved?"

"You know ... just meetings and riding, nothing much."

Pablo looked questionably at Marcus; he knew different, but he would leave it at that for now. "Please don't let on to Momma that you are involved with bikers, okay?"

"Sure, why would I?"

"Hey, do you know what day it is?" Pablo said.

Marcus looked over at Pab and then down at his watch. It was the anniversary of their Uncle George's death.

"Oh fuck, I had totally forgotten. I've been so out of it lately," Marcus said. "We need to go out to Uncle George's gravesite. Do you think we should invite Momma along?"

"Well, you know she has had a very tough time dealing with George's death, even now, I still don't think she's ready to go out there," Pablo said.

They finished their cigarettes and went into the house. Marcus disappeared into his room for a few minutes and then returned.

Rosalia was busy cleaning the kitchen when they walked in. "You guys seem in a much better mood. What's up?"

"Not much. Marcus and I are going to head up to the cemetery to visit Uncle George's gravesite."

"Oh, I see," her eyes were sad. "My dear sons, I should have said something today about it," Rosalia said.

Pablo could see the tears welling up in her eyes. He went over to her and gave her a comforting hug. "It's okay, Momma, we understand. You don't mind us taking off for a bit, do you? I mean, you'll be okay?"

Rosalia nodded her head as if to say it was okay. They gave her a kiss and then proceeded out the front door. It was already after 8:00 P.M., and Marcus still had to meet Davis that evening about the drug deal. *How was he going to get out of there now, now that Pablo knew he was involved? Pablo would really know something was up at that hour.*

Marcus and Pablo got on their motorcycles and headed off towards town. The cemetery was about twenty minutes north of town. It would take them about forty-five minutes in total to get there. It wouldn't leave much time for Marcus to ditch Pablo and get back to the alley to meet Davis.

Marcus and Pablo had made a promise to each other that they would visit their uncle's gravesite every year on the anniversary of his death.

As they stood over the gravesite, Marcus reached inside his vest and pulled out the book 'Riders of Reason.' He looked over at Pablo, and he nodded. Marcus felt it was now time to let it rest. Marcus passed the book to Pablo, with a pen, and Pablo signed the book and returned it to Marcus. Marcus had already signed the inside. He placed the book on top of his Uncle's headstone. They sat down on the grass for what seemed to be an hour, until they heard a loud rumble. Pablo turned his head to the left and noticed two bikes had pulled up beside theirs. They stood up. The men walked towards Marcus and Pablo. It was Boss and another man. Marcus and Pablo couldn't help but stare at these men. Marcus knew Boss, but he wasn't sure about the other man. As Marcus and Pablo watched them, they briefly forgot about the book.

Boss put out his hand towards Pablo. Pablo hesitated and reached out and shook his hand; he vaguely recognized Boss from the hospital. Boss gave Marcus a brotherly hug, and then he looked down at the headstone. He took out a piece of paper from his pocket. "You men don't mind?" he asked Pablo and Marcus.

"No, not at all," Marcus said. Pablo was sceptical.

Marcus and Pablo stepped back a bit and were silent. Boss removed his doo-rag and read:

Here lies our brother
Taken too soon before his time
A member not forgotten
Nor mentioned for his crime.

We will always stand in honour
Every year, on this day forth
And show our love and faithfulness
For a brother who has worth.

Boss took a breath. Marcus had never seen this side of him before. All he had seen is the tough, rough exterior.

Even though our bond was cut
Our brotherhood still lives
We trust that you are riding free
Among members in the skies.

I lay down this patch we've made
For a man who showed us pride
And wear one on the back of me
In remembrance of you——Let's ride!

After Boss finished reciting the poem he had written for their uncle, he placed the piece of paper inside the book, but left a corner of it sticking out. He didn't want the book to fall into anyone else's hands, so he lit the piece of paper with his lighter. The book went up in flames. Nobody said anything. Marcus and Pablo stood there in shock, while they watched it burn down to nothing but ashes. They didn't know why Boss had done this, but there weren't about to ask any questions either. *Maybe it's for the best*, Pablo thought.

When Boss was done, he asked Marcus and Pablo if they wanted to join them for a drink, to honour their uncle. How could they not say yes? Pablo was satisfied that burning the book would give them some closure, but he was very uneasy about these men.

The four bikes fired up. Boss instructed Marcus and Pablo to ride side-by-side behind them. Marcus was used to riding in procession like this with them, but Pablo wasn't. He momentarily forgot about Boss and was hypnotized by the overwhelming feeling as they rode down the main road with these two bikers in front of them. He did feel it to be an honour.

They pulled into the parking lot, and Marcus and Pablo followed them into the pub.

When they entered the pub, there were a few other bikers sitting around a table. This was the table they joined. Marcus noticed Davis was one of the others at the table. He hoped that Davis wasn't going to say anything about the drug deal while Pablo was with them.

They all sat down and ordered some drinks. There was little conversation among them. Davis called Marcus to come over and talk with him. Marcus got up from his chair and sat down in the empty one beside Davis. Pablo watched intently. After a few minutes, Marcus got up and sat back down beside Pablo.

"Everything okay?" Pablo asked quietly.

"Sure, just fine."

Boss rose to his feet. "Brothers, this is a toast to George 'Whiskey' Gomez!" He raised his drink with the others. All the rest of the bikers raised their drinks and hit them together. "Our brother!"

The bikers knew that even though George had been let go from the club years ago, he would always remain as part of the family.

After Marcus and Pablo finished their drinks, Pablo decided it was time they headed out. It was getting late, and their momma would be extremely worried by now. He nudged his brother, as if to say 'let's go.' Marcus knew it was getting close to midnight now, and he wouldn't be able to leave. He grabbed his jacket and the two of them went outside for a moment, avoiding Davis' puzzled stare.

"Look, I can't go just yet. I have to talk with Davis about

something. I'll meet you back at home," Marcus said.

Pablo was worried about Marcus. "Are you sure, Marcus? Is everything okay?"

"Yes," but he avoided Pablo's eyes.

"Well ... alright. Do me a favour, and keep your head up," Pablo said. "I'll be waiting for you at home."

They gave each other a pat on the back and Marcus went into the bar. He returned to his seat at the table. The other bikers were getting louder by the minute.

Pablo got on his bike. He knew it wasn't the right thing to do, but he rode away from the bar, but stayed close enough so that he could see when the bikers left. He needed to follow them and make sure Marcus was alright. He realized he was taking a big chance, but he had to do this.

He parked his bike in the next parking lot and remained there, quietly. He hoped they weren't going to be too much longer, as the temperature was dropping and it was getting a bit chilly. He lit up a cigarette and took in a long drag. *Why did Marcus have to get involved?*

Davis looked at his watch. It was 11:30 P.M. "Okay, boys, it's time to roll!" They all got up from their seats and put their jackets on. It wasn't going to be just Davis and Marcus this time; there would be at least twenty of them going. Davis figured he had better have backup, just in case. They bustled out of the bar.

Pablo quickly flicked his butt out onto the pavement as he heard loud voices over by the bikes.

Thank god. I never thought they would come out of there. He carefully watched them, and hoped they didn't see him. He wondered how he was going to follow them without being seen. He imagined they were good at keeping people at a distance.

Once they all had their leathers on, it was almost impossible for Pablo to tell which one was Marcus. The bikes pulled out of the parking lot. Pablo waited until the last bike pulled out and then he rode behind them. He followed the bikes until they were close to the alley. Davis decided that they had better not pull into the alley this time, because they may need to get away quickly. They rode past the alley and parked their bikes a few streets down. Pablo followed as close to them as possible and watched where they pulled off. He continued down another block, so they wouldn't spot him. He then dismounted and walked to the corner. He could hear the commotion of the bikers as he got closer to the alley. He waited for a few minutes until he noticed that the voices got lower, almost silent. He then peered around the corner. Carefully, he walked along the wall on the right hand side. He continued until he could hear the voices again. They sounded muffled, so he assumed they were inside somewhere. He stopped at the far corner of the building he was beside, and listened carefully. Suddenly, he heard rumbling behind him. He turned around and saw some bikes heading straight towards him. His heart jumped into his throat. He wanted to run, but there was nowhere to go. So he stood there shaking. He hadn't done anything wrong, but he knew by the looks of the bikes that were coming in, that he was not in good company. The head biker, Torch, looked directly at him, and then stopped his bike.

"Who are you?" Torch said gruffly.

Pablo was lost for words. He was going to say something but thought better of it and just stood there. Torch motioned to the others to park their bikes. He dismounted his.

"Are you one of them?" he asked. Pablo didn't know what to say. He thought that if he said no, he could be in more trouble than if he said yes. "Yes."

"I see. Well, let's get this over with then." He motioned for the other bikers to follow him, and nodded to Pablo. Pablo decided that he meant for him to follow, so he did.

The bikers and Pablo headed in through the broken window of the building. The voices of the other bikers were now louder. They went into the room with the rest. Pablo tried to stay hidden from the others, but it was impossible, because they pushed him ahead of them. Once they were in the room, Torch gave Pablo a good shove and he ended up in front of Davis and Boss.

"Who's this?" Davis said. "And what is he doing here?"

Marcus turned around and saw his brother's face. "Pablo!" he said under his breath. *What the hell is he doing here?* he thought.

"He said he was with you guys," Torch said.

Boss looked among his members. "He's not with us."

"This is bullshit! You were warned to come alone and not to bring anyone else!" Torch was pissed.

"Look, let's talk about this," Davis said. He moved closer to Torch. "He's harmless, look at him."

Torch looked Pablo over. "How do we know he's not a narc!?"

Pablo had no clue as to what he just walked in on, but he knew it wasn't good.

Marcus was praying that Pablo wasn't going to say anything— especially that he was his brother.

"Well, in any case, there is no way we can finish this deal," Torch said to Davis.

Boss pushed the suitcases of cocaine towards the wall and moved closer to Davis.

"Look this should have been over by now. We are wasting time here. The longer we're here, the more chances are that the Feds will arrive!" Boss hollered.

"That isn't our problem, now is it? You are the one that went against the deal, not us!" Torch and Davis were now face-to-face.

Suddenly, before Davis knew what happened, the other members of 'Riders of Reason' had burst out from behind him and were attacking the other bikers.

"Stop!" Boss hollered. "This isn't going to solve anything!"

Pablo sneaked in behind Marcus, who also was trying not to get involved in the commotion. Marcus whispered to Pablo, "Just keep quiet, don't say a word."

Davis was feeling the pressure and there was no way ... he reached towards his back, but no sooner had he moved his hand, that he was suddenly face-first on the damp cement floor, with the heel of a size twelve Milwaukee boot pressed into the back of his neck. Torch bore his foot down with more pressure on Davis' neck, until he pleaded for him to stop. Torch gave it a few seconds and with one last push, he backed off and glanced over at Marcus. Shivers of fear rolled down Marcus' spine. He said nothing.

Boss had come up behind Torch and pushed him against the wall. Two other bikers, on either side helped Boss hold him. Boss then continued to knee Torch in the groin. He buckled over in agony. Marcus and Pablo didn't know what to do. Marcus knew he should be helping, but was afraid to.

After a few minutes of fists flying, and knees and feet crushing, there was a loud *bang*. The door to the building crashed open, and there stood five Federal police officers. They stood with guns pointed at the bikers. At the same time, one of the bikers had set off a smoke bomb in the room. The bikers started coughing and gagging. Davis got to his feet and grabbed a hold of Marcus and Pablo. He then motioned to the other members, among the smoke, and commotion, and led them into the room where the ventilation shaft was. They climbed up inside, and crawled through the tight enclosure, until they arrived at the end. Davis pulled out his knife and shoved it in between the grate and the wall, until it loosened. He pushed the grate hard, and it fell to the ground. They jumped down onto the pavement, which was the front of the building and scoped the area. There were two empty police cars out front, so they guessed they hadn't called for backup just yet. They ran down to the next building and climbed up the fire escape ladder to the roof of the building. From there they ran to the other side, and leapt over to the building beside it. The buildings in this area were built very close together, so they had the advantage of being able to get over to the next one. They crossed a few of the buildings, and then climbed down another fire escape ladder. They were now far enough away from where the others were. They would wait here for a bit until it calmed down, and they could make a run for their bikes.

Once they were able to get to their bikes, they rode off in the opposite direction. Davis hoped that the officers had nailed the other bikers good, but he had a gut feeling that this wasn't over. Marcus and Pablo followed Davis until they reached the clubhouse. They parked the bikes in the back parking lot and rushed inside.

Davis was out of breath. Everything was going so wrong.

Davis took Pablo aside. "Who are you?"

Pablo looked at Davis and then at Marcus. "I'm Marcus' brother, well actually his step-brother."

"Is this true, Marcus?" Davis looked over at Marcus.

Marcus wasn't able to look at Davis.

"Marcus!" Davis grabbed him by his arm and turned him around. "Is this true?"

"Yes, sir." Marcus shyly turned his head towards Davis.

"Why, why would you involve others, when you knew this was a big deal, especially non-members?!"

"Look Davis, I never told him—honest." Marcus needed to think of something and quick.

"Well, shit Marcus. How did he find us then?"

Marcus didn't have a clue. "I don't know, Davis."

Davis sat down and thought for a few minutes. What was he going to do? The heat was on them, and now he had a non-member to deal with, who also knew what was happening.

"We are going to have to meet again, soon. For now, you guys head home, and do not say anything to anyone!" Davis rose from his chair and pulled out a cold beer from the fridge. His stomach wasn't feeling well at all. He had to figure out what to do.

chapter

21

MARCUS AND PABLO had kept a low profile for the last few days, for their sake as well as their momma's; she didn't need to know what was going on, at least not yet. They rode their motorcycles out to the local bar to meet with Davis. He was already there when they arrived. Marcus spotted Davis, but he wasn't alone. Boss was also there. They sat down at the table across from them.

"I'm sorry for having to call you in Pablo, but I don't have a choice, now that you know what's going on.

"As you both know, the deal didn't go well. There was over 80lbs of cocaine in that transaction, and you don't want to know how much that is worth. Unfortunately, I have to do something to cover everyone's ass."

Marcus looked over at Pablo. He was confused. Pablo was not sure what Davis was saying; he was still pretty much in the dark about things.

"What do you mean, Davis?" Marcus asked. Pablo leaned in closer.

"The heat is on us, sons. We have no choice now—but to leave the country."

"What?" Marcus said. He looked over at Pablo, who was now looking around to make sure no one was listening.

"Leave the country? Why?" Marcus picked up the beer in front of him and downed the rest in one gulp. He put the bottle down.

"I'm sorry. But remember the oath you signed, Marcus?" Davis said.

Pablo looked at Marcus, "Oath? Don't tell me you signed an oath!"

Marcus recalled the papers. "Yes." He looked away from Pablo.

"When Marcus was accepted into the club, he had to sign some papers. Those papers were a promise, which meant that he would have to do anything to keep the members of the 'club' safe, no matter what happened," Davis explained.

Pablo wasn't sure he liked what he was hearing. He recalled what his Uncle George had said about the oath.

"All our brothers are in jeopardy now, and it's up to me to make sure they're all safe. If not, the entire club will be brought down to their knees, and every member will be imprisoned."

Davis placed his hand on Pablo's arm. "Son, you *both* will have to leave the country. I have made arrangements for when you leave here."

"What? What do you mean by both of us?" Pablo said.

"I have no choice Pablo, you know too much," Davis said.

"What, we have to leave today?" Marcus said.

"Marcus," Davis said, "we have to keep this quiet." Davis looked around the bar. Luckily there weren't too many in the bar close to them. The bartender glanced over at Davis. Davis spotted him and said, "Once again!" and made a circular gesture over the table. The bartender nodded and brought the men another round of beer. Marcus turned his head away, so that the bartender wouldn't see his face.

"So, what do we do then?" Pablo asked.

Marcus couldn't believe what he was hearing. He kept shaking his head. *What about their momma? She would be devastated*, he thought.

"Hand me your IDs," Davis said.

Marcus dug out his wallet and tossed it over at Davis. Davis removed all the items relating to his real name and then handed it back to Marcus. He did the same with Pablo's. Davis passed both their IDs over to Boss.

"Okay, Boss. Hurry, and meet us back at the clubhouse," Davis said.

Boss got up quickly. Marcus and Pablo sat still. They didn't know what to say, but they needed to trust Davis.

"Now look, I am really hoping this will all be cleared up in a matter of months," Davis repeated. "Marcus, you will need to hand over your vest, as well."

Marcus removed his leather vest and hesitantly passed it to Davis. Neither one of them liked what was happening.

"Davis, could you do us a favour?" asked Pablo.

"Sure, if I can," Davis said, while he stuffed the vest into a bag.

"Please let our mother know we're okay. I cannot tell you how stressed she's been over the years with everything else that has happened. Just let her know we're alive and safe?"

"I'll do what I can. But I can't promise," Davis said. "I have to leave the country as well, but I am heading to Mexico. Canada will be much safer for you two."

"Canada? Do you know how far away that is?" Marcus said, under his breath.

"Yes, but the authorities won't be able to touch you there," Davis said. "Hopefully everything will blow over within a couple of months. If not, you will have to remain there until you hear from me."

"What about the others?" Marcus asked.

"Everyone who was involved will be doing the same. We have to make sure all grounds are covered," Davis said. "It will be nice when this is all over."

"No kidding," Pablo said.

Davis reached into his pocket and pulled out some cash. "Here, this should keep you going for a couple of months. You both will have to get employment while in Weyburn and live as much of a normal life as possible until this is over."

Pablo and Marcus reached out for the money and placed it in their wallets.

"Both of you have been set up with different living arrangements.

The addresses will be on your new IDs, which Boss will give to you once we get back to the clubhouse. Okay, your flight leaves in three hours, so let's finish our beer and get your bikes to the clubhouse, and locked up. Then I will drive you to the airport."

Marcus and Pablo rose from their seats and went out to the parking lot. They got on their bikes and followed Davis. Marcus wanted to take off and head home, but he knew he better not, not this time. They drove in a kind of daze. They followed Davis' truck into the lot behind the clubhouse. There was an old abandoned garage on the far corner of the property. They headed there. Davis jumped out of his pickup and opened the garage door. Once opened, he looked in. There were already ten bikes inside. Pablo wanted to ask Davis questions, but instead he just drove his bike inside. Marcus parked alongside him. Davis removed the license plates and took their keys. "When you return, you will get these back." Davis locked the garage, and they waited for Boss to show up.

Boss arrived a few minutes later. He parked his bike and walked up to Davis.

"Did you get them done?" Davis asked.

Boss nodded and pulled out some documents from inside his vest. He placed them down on the hood of the truck in front of Marcus and Pablo. "I have new identifications, passports and addresses in Weyburn, Saskatchewan."

Davis peeked over Boss' shoulders. "Impressive, my man! Impressive! I still don't know how you can pull this off in such a short time, but I really don't want to know your secrets," Davis said, and laughed.

Boss let out an evil chuckle.

Marcus picked his ID up. A photo of him was on it, but beside the photo, it read the name Rick Statler. He looked over at Pablo and then back at Davis. Pablo's name was now Mike Williams.

"What? We're not even related?" Marcus said. "This is crap!" He tossed the ID and documents at Davis. "Keep this shit. I'm not going anywhere!" Marcus turned around to leave, but felt Davis' hand grip his forearm. "Marcus, I know how you're feeling. I promise, it won't be long."

Pablo nodded at Marcus. Pablo wasn't going to fight Davis; he understood the situation a little clearer than Marcus did, maybe it was because of his talks with his uncle.

"See you later, Davis," Boss said. He patted Pablo and Marcus on the shoulders, and then headed for his bike. It was only seconds before his bike was rumbling and heading out of the parking lot.

"Okay, let's get you guys to the airport," Davis said.

They put their new IDs and passports into their pockets.

Davis opened the passenger door of the truck. "Get in." Marcus and Pablo got into the truck. It was a snug fit; it felt muggy and claustrophobic. "We'll be at the airport in about forty-five minutes," Davis said. "Just relax, it will all work out." *Relax, my ass!* Marcus thought. Davis lit a cigar and opened his window. He didn't like the idea of shipping them off, but he had to in order to keep them safe. He hoped in time they would forgive him.

epilogue

MARCUS (RICK) AND PABLO (MIKE) had settled into their new identities and lives easier than they'd imagined they would. When they first arrived in Weyburn, Saskatchewan, everything was set up for them. They both managed to secure employment and tried to live somewhat normal lives.

Rick met a peppy girl by the name of Stacy O'Brien, and it wasn't long before they fell in love and were married. Rick had purchased a motorcycle for Stacy and they rode together. They had a great relationship, until about two years later when Rick was contacted and threatened because of his past. He was ordered to cut all personal ties. This meant he had to divorce Stacy. He sold the bikes, and did his best to cover his trail. As far as anyone knew, he never rode and wasn't interested in motorcycles. He did all this to protect Stacy; he didn't want her hurt. He wished he could explain things to her, but he was ordered not to. The less information she knew the better it would be for them both.

Rick moved into a small apartment and led a very secluded life after that. He spent many nights waiting by the phone for that call from Davis, that would tell him that all was okay to return to Argentina.

Mike and Rick didn't communicate much after Rick had been threatened. They pretty much went their own way, which was probably for the best for Mike. He worried about Rick, but at the same time, he needed to take care of himself.

Mike often thought about his Momma back in Argentina and

how she was coping. It had been a few years since he had seen her. He prayed she would forgive him once they returned. Mike had joined a riding club called 'Wings of the World.' This club was different than the one that Rick had belonged to in Argentina. It was a family oriented club, but family meant something different; it was truly family and there was nothing illegal about what they did.

The weather couldn't have been better for a group ride that day. It was just past 6:00 P.M. when Mike turned off to head towards home. He pulled out of the group formation, and waved to the other members as he peeled off down the fast lane towards the outskirts of Weyburn.

Just as he passed the next intersection towards the bridge, his bike began acting up. It wasn't performing the way it should. He geared down as he approached the bridge. As he pulled off the road, he slowed down cautiously on the loose gravel. Once his bike was steady, he placed his feet down and lowered the kickstand. He got off the bike and looked it over.

Odd. It appears to be fine. He remained there momentarily, scratching his head. He couldn't understand what may have gone wrong. He sat down on a nearby rock and pondered over the bike. After he finished his cigarette, he flicked it out onto the paved road, stood up and got back on his bike.

He slowly rolled on the throttle and changed gears until he reached fourth gear. The bike was cruising down the highway normally now. He started to accelerate around the next corner when he suddenly saw the front end of a car heading towards him. He pressed his rear brake with the toe of his right foot, and pulled in the right hand lever. The front brake wasn't working! He pressed down harder on the rear brake; the back tire locked up! The bike buckled and the ass-end slid out from underneath him, swinging in the direction of the car. The car struck the back of the bike and twisted it so hard in the opposite direction, that it flew up in the air, bounced off the asphalt again and landed near the concrete barrier on the other side of the highway. Mike was thrown off the bike, and he landed hard face-first on the concrete beneath him—everything went black.